ACORNS IN A SKILLET:

STORIES OF RACECRAFT IN AMERICA

by
Tony Lindsay

ACORNS IN A SKILLET:
STORIES OF RACECRAFT IN AMERICA

by
Tony Lindsay

PROSPERITY PUBLICATIONS
San Antonio, Texas

PROSPERITY PUBLICATIONS
510 Ramsey Road
Suite #3
San Antonio, Texas 78216

ISBN: 978-0-9863740-1-2

Cover Art
Graphic Art: Larry Cope
Inside text design: Tracy Harden
Printed in the United States of America

TABLE OF CONTENTS

- ONE -
STOP AND FRISK

Last night, when he came home after school and work, he was tired. Randy took his first midterm exam on the college level, and this morning he felt good about the unknown results. The English test had been difficult, but he studied hard the weeks prior and the night before. He was certain of a good grade. This confidence had him smiling while waiting for the bus. Most of his buddies and some of the people he worked with said he was wasting his time going to school.

His oldest friend Jacob told him, "Man the dice have already been rolled for Black dudes like us. It is messenger, cabby, restaurants, janitor, or the streets. That is where dudes like us get our money." Those were the words Jacob told Randy when he went to the G.E.D. program offered through the library. When he fished the program and passed the test, Jacob told him, "Man you tripping, if you think the white man got anything for you but jail."

What Randy saw around him agreed with Jacob, most of their friends, their brothers, and fathers had done time in jail, but Randy knew black men did live without jail. He saw them in the subway, on buses, he watched them going to work at jobs not on street corners. The first time he voted was to help one become president of the United States. Jacob was right and wrong, and last night's test, like passing the G.E.D. exam, made Randy think Jacob was more wrong than right.

Today he had to work seven hours inside the golden arches before he went to school. The sun wasn't up, but he and six other people at the bus stop were. He yawns and adjusts his book bag on his shoulder.

"Now cut that out young blood, you know those are contagious. I see you yawning then I'ma start, and the next you know I'ma think about going back upstairs, calling in, and getting back in my bed next to the Mrs."

Randy laughs and shakes his head no, "Mr. Peters, who are you trying to fool? There are two things that are stopping that from happening. First, you haven't missed a day of work in twenty three as you have told me many times over theses three months that I have been catching the bus with you, and second, Mrs. Peters just finished her shift at the hospital, and she is not about to have you coming back in the bed disturbing her rest. So Sir, I am going to keep on yawning, and you can join me if you want, but that bus coming up the Avenue has a seat for you just like does everybody else out here."

The two ladies standing behind them start laughing too, "Randy, it is too early for all that truth this morning. You should let Mr. Peters have his little fantasy. He can dream about going back upstairs if he wants too," one of them snickers.

"I ain't dreamin'. I am a grown man. I can go back upstairs if I want to," he huffs. The brakes on the bus squeal as it comes to a stop in front of the crowd. "But, I don't want to," Mr. Peters climbs the bus' stairs, "Mornin' Malcolm," he says to the driver.

"Good morning, Mr. Peters, when are you going to let the ladies on first?"

"When they get out here first," Mr. Peters answers flashing his bus pass.

Randy who has stepped aside allowing the ladies to enter sees police squad car lights approaching the bus. His stomach tightens and flips; he wishes he had gotten on the bus like Mr. Peters. The squad car blocks the bus and puts a spot light on those remaining outside of it.

"Hey, you with the book-bag, hold it right there!" comes from the speaker of the squad car.

Randy takes a step toward the steps of the bus.

"I said hold it!"

He stops, and the others walk pass him boarding the bus. He would have done the same. No one wants a hassle with the police. Both officers are out of the squad approaching him. One has drawn his pistol.

"Step away from the bus."

Randy does.

"What is in the book-bag?"

The officer with his pistol holstered asks.

"Books and my lunch."

"Books? Drop it to the ground."

Randy lets the book-bag fall from his shoulder to the ground.

When he does, the officer with the holstered gun is upon him.

He trips Randy to ground causing his chin to hit the sidewalk, which forces his teeth into tongue. His mouth fills with blood. The officer handcuffs him while his partner goes through Randy's book bag.

The officer who cuffed him is going through his pockets. He strips off Randy's shoes and socks and is going thorough both; finding nothing he puts on latex gloves and forces his hand down the back of Randy's pants and around to his crotch area. Randy is still laying face-down on the sidewalk.

"Anything in the book-bag?" He yells to his partner.

"Just books and a sandwich."

The officer that searched him un-cuffs him. The other officer throws his book-bag to him. They return to their squad car and pull off allowing the bus to leave.

Malcolm, the bus driver calls, "Randy"

He sits up, spits out blood and then stands.

Behind the bus, Jacob pulls up in his Chevy with the music blaring. Randy waves the bus on and walks to the Chevy.

- TWO -
HOME GROWN

It was three o'clock in the afternoon. The blinds that hung in front of the room's only window were open. The afternoon sun flooded the studio apartment. It was a bright room without the sun with the sun it beamed. The cherry wood bureau, table, and chairs gleamed in the sun's light. The walls and kitchen appliances were eggshell white. The chrome sink claimed as much sun as the cherry wood and bright walls. The room held the sun.

In the center of the room was a queen-sized bed. The frame of the bed was anchored to a cherry wood headboard. The frame held a box spring, a coil mattress, and Luther Armstrong. Luther laid atop the bed that was made in military fashion. A fitted sheet, a cover sheet, and a brown cotton spread covered the coil mattress. Luther Armstrong lay across the bed grinning at the ceiling.

His two hundred seventy pound, five foot ten inch frame covered a large portion of the bed. A white undershirt covered his muscular torso. His bottom half was covered by a pair of white sweatpants.

His feet were in a pair of white high-top leather gym shoes. He wore no underwear or socks.

The grin across his face was due to a dilemma he solved. The problem was his hair. He wanted it to make a statement. He wanted it to say, fuck you. He tried braids, hair relaxer, and curls. None said it quite loud enough. When he woke this morning, the answer was clear. He cut it all off. He was so pleased with the image in the mirror. All he could do was grin. The bald head was what he needed to complete his plan.

Today, August fourth, he put it all together. Reform school, prison, and the state mental hospital were all training grounds for today. Reform school taught him how to say yes when he was screaming no on the inside. Prison taught him how to say no when he wanted to scream yes. The state mental hospital taught him how to grin. Today, he wouldn't say yes or no. Today he would say fuck you. Today, for the first time in his life, he followed his plan: not the teacher's, the social worker's, or the gang's, his. The plan began in his mind five weeks ago. It was his first session with his parole officer.

For the first time in his life, he realized his life wasn't his fault. Until that session, he always thought his misery was due to making wrong choices. He blamed himself for his poor reading skills. He blamed himself for joining a gang. He blamed himself for stealing. He blamed himself for being crazy. Others did, why shouldn't he? He accepted the consequences of his actions with no complaints. He accepted the labels people applied to him: dumb, thief, drug addict, habitual criminal, and crazy. He was what people told him he was. He was sitting across the desk from his parole officer when a new label was applied.

"Institutionalized, that's what you've become Mr. Armstrong."

He didn't know what the word meant, but he knew it was bad because term was applied to him. He asked the young black female parole officer . . . who institutionalized him? She told him the system. He asked whose system?

"Society's."

"Whose society?"

"Ours . . . well . . . mostly the white man's."

The light went on in his mind that day and stayed on. The white man - the white man's society - the white man's rules - he was a Black man. It wasn't his fault. He was in the wrong society. He was the wrong color for this society. If it were a Black society, the white man would be given a poor education. The white man would be dumb, crazy, a habitual criminal, and institutionalized.

This society, white society, cheated him. White society owed him. It wasn't his fault. How was he supposed to play by their rules? They were white rules. He was Black. No one explained the rules until he broke them. It wasn't fair. They cheated him, and they owed him. They owed him for all the good things they kept away from him, a good education and a good job. They owed him for the life he didn't have. He was Black in a white society. It wasn't his fault. But today, he would make it right.

Luther Armstrong rose from the neatly made bed still grinning. He walked over to the cherry wood bureau and opened the top drawer. The drawer held one butcher's knife, a steak knife, and a roll of invisible tape. He pulled up his white undershirt and placed both knives behind the elastic waistband of his white sweatpants. He pulled his undershirt down concealing the knife handles. He held the tape in his hand. Still grinning, he turned and left the bright apartment.

Once on the street, he walked erect and deliberate. The grin was plastered on his face. It would be the first one. The first one that made eye contact - the first one that said something to him - the first one he heard - the first one he smelled - it would be the first one.

A Mexican, close.

An Arab, close.

A Black, fuck.

A white, little, blond haired boy with blue eyes: bingo.

The work was harder than Luther expected. The kill was easy enough, but the work; the work was much harder. Concentration pushed the grin from his face. It was messy delicate work; most definitely not to be done in an alley, but an alley was all he had. The trick was to find pieces big enough to wrap. Luther cursed himself for not bringing a pair of scissors, but how was he to know? He'd never done it before. White men knew how to do it, but they knew most things; it's their society.

The work took longer than Luther expected, but once finished, the grin returned to his face. Every part of his exposed skin was right now. Everywhere he looked, it was right. His arms were right, his fingers were right, his face was right, he was right.

No more misery. Everything would be right because he was right. He walked from the alley with confidence and pride. Life was going to be better now. No one would dare call him dumb or crazy. With just one look, everyone would know he was right.

Now he could say fuck you without looking away. He could say fuck you the way white men said it. He could say fuck you nigger and stare a Black man straight in the eye. After all, he was right now. He was part of society. No more black man in the wrong society. He was in the right society. No more unexplained rules. He walked from that alley reborn. He was right and white as any white man. Sure, he needed tape to hold the right skin on, but he would fix that. Now since he was white, he knew he should have used crazy glue.

- Three -
A Church Morning

He has placed his hand on the small of my back while opening the church door for me. The very first sight I see is Sister Mildred's wide pink chiffon covered backside pointing at us from the
top stairs. She is stepping up into the lobby, and being behind her at
the bottom of the stairs all I see are pink ruffles ahead.

When I look to Henry, to see if he notices her ruffled layered
hips, his blue eyes are on me, and he is smiling. Dang, I love this
man.

"The church is closer than I thought. It didn't take us twenty
minutes to get here." Henry says opening his suit jacket while allowing me the steps. Sister Mildred has rustled herself from view, so I
begin stepping up the stairs.

"I don't know if it was the short distance or the speed you drove
that got us here so fast," I say.

When I get to the top of the staircase, I step into bight morning sun beaming through the high church windows. The glass isn't

stained, so the sun fills the lobby. It feels like a personal welcoming, and I love it. A crowd for the first service, even on Easter Sunday, is rarity. Daddy will be pleased with the crowd.

The ushers have opened the doors of the sanctuary, and the noisy colorful congregation is moving through them. Little girls in yellow, pink and white dresses with clacking black patent leather shoes are catching my eyes. I hear mothers directing: "stop running," "get over here," "pull that up," "tuck that in," and I have missed it all; the sights and sounds of families coming to praise warms my spirit.

I am doing the right thing.

From behind me Henry asks, "Which way?"

"To the left," I tell him. My brother always sits to the left of the main aisle, and we will sit with him this morning. The congregation is moving swiftly through the doors. Henry and I are walking behind a young family; I recognize the mother, Meredith Stewart now Meredith Anderson. She and I we were youth ushers together. She is now a mother of three; the oldest, a girl, looks to be about six. The last time I saw Meredith she was getting married that was about seven years ago. I have been absent from this church a little over six years. The daughter has on a bright purple dress and is directing, no, pushing her younger brothers through the doors. If memory serves me right, Meredith likes to sit in the third row with her mother-in-law, Mrs. Anderson.

I spot my brother sitting with his husband Mathew; my mother married them in this church eight years ago despite my father's and the deacon board's protest, but she is the pastor of the church, and the congregation loves her, so she is able to do what she thinks is God's will.

I love this church, but my theft of sixty three hundred dollars from the missionary account kept me away. The repayment is in my purse in cash. My parents and brother told me the money wasn't important; they and the church wanted me back.

I am being recognized while Henry and I are walking up the side aisle. People are waving, so I am returning waves, nods, and smiles.

Henry reaches back for my hand; he grabs it and squeezes it.

We stop at my brother's row, and he still hasn't seen us.

"Juanita?" a voice from behind calls.

I turn and see Mother York, the church treasure who discovered my theft. She reported my deed to deacon's board before she told my mother. I command my face to smile and will my arms to rise and open in a hugging gesture. Mother Yorks doesn't hesitant to step into the embrace. She smells like Ben Gay and green rubbing alcohol.

"It is so good to see you back, Juanita."

Her hug is tight enough to make me believe her words. For a skinny old lady, she has considerable strength.

"It's good to be back Mother York."

"Praise him, we prayed you back into this church," she says into my ear breaking the embrace.

I don't doubt that my mother and other saints prayed me back, but it's hard for me to imagine Mother York bending an arthritic knee for me. We nod and smile again at each other and proceed to our seats.

My brother and his husband see us now.

"Hey Henry and Juanita," my brother gives us his toothy smile.

"Jeremy, Mathew," Henry speaks but lets me enter the row first.

My brother, Jeremy, stands and we embrace.

"I saw the Wicked Witch of York stalking you from the lobby; she pushed past people to get to you."

"Stop it," I say because Mother York is sitting in the row directly behind us, and she could easily her him. My brother has never been nice when speaking of church mothers; I think it was all the swats on the butt and ear pulling they gave him as a little boy.

"It's true. She stalked you." Jeremy says.

We sit grinning at each other like we use to do we when were kids. He is four years older, but I kept him out of trouble at church. He was the bad preacher's kid, not me. Looking around, I estimate about seventy-five people in the sanctuary; my mother held first service when only five members came despite the deacon's, which included my father's, protest. Seventy-five members is a long way from five. My mother has more faith than any person I know; she trusts completely in God and believes he will provide all her needs. Jeremy's husband Mathew leans forward and looks at Henry and says, "Henry, I would like you to represent me in my divorce." He is speaking over me and my brother to Henry, and he is not whispering, not yelling, but he's not being discrete, or as my mother would say not using "a church voice."

"On the grounds of adultery," he continues still looking at Henry waiting for an answer.

I look at my brother, and he has the same toothy grin on his face that he greeted us with. His big brown eyes, innocent looking to most people, are telling me he is guilty. As a child he told me, "grown people believes lies when you look them in the eye," so he always looked grown people in the eye when he was lying, adults would be fooled, but I wouldn't be. I saw the yes when he was say ing no: yes, I took a dollar out of the collection plate – yes, I ate the cookies on the saints table – yes, I smoked a cigarette in Deacon's Hall bathroom - yes, I pulled the church fire alarm, - yes, I cheated on my husband.

My fiancés, Henry's, clear blue eyes dart from Mathew to me to back to Mathew, "We should talk after service." My lawyer fiancé suggests in a discrete church voice. The tips of his ears and the base of his neck are turning red.

"Why?" Mathew sits prone. "The other adulterer is right here; sitting right over there with family," he nods his head like a pointing finger.

I try not to look at who he is nodding his head towards, but I can't help myself. The only family in the direction of the nod is Dr. Anderson and Meredith, no. I look at my brother who is still grinning, yes.

"Oh my God, I'm leaving," I tell my brother. He merely raises his eyes brows and keeps smiling. The organ begins to play and the choir is entering the stand from both sides singing, "What a Friend I have in Jesus." I am looking at the Combined Church Choir instead of my brother. I would leave because I hate confrontation, but my reason for being here is not about my brother.

"We're not leaving, are we?" Henry asks in response to my statement. He knows why we are here, and how important making this amends is to me.

"No," I answer reaching for and holding on to his hand again. My eyes are pulled to the harmonizing choir. I sang in the Combined Church Choir from my thirteenth birthday until my theft at twen ty-six. I never sang in the Teen Choir or the Woman's Choir just the Combined Church Choir. There were about ten of us that only song in the combined choir; Dr. Anderson, Vincent, was one of the ten. And . . . Vincent was also who I lost my virginity to: me and Meredith both. He was cute, smart, quiet and never kissed and told; it was us girls that told.

I cut my eyes over to my brother who is no longer smiling, but he is looking straight ahead and not at his husband, Mathew. I lean to his ear, "But . . . Vincent is not gay?"

My brother's big toothy grin returns, "One mustn't make assumptions." He says with his big brown eyes still on the choir.
I lean away from him and sit up straight. My mother enters the pulpit with the choir still singing; she is wearing a white cassock trimmed in purple. She must have rolled her hair to the back last night because her light brown curls are flowing back and hanging midway down her back. She does a little holy dance to rhythm of the choir in front of the oak podium, and the congregation stands and claps.

Others throughout the church join my mother in her holy dance; the organ and the drums take the lead and the church is in a joyous uproar. We are all standing and in some type of motion, but everyone is not joyous; Mathew isn't. His glare remains on the Andersons.
He raises his hands overhead, and my attention focuses on his perfectly manicured and clear polished nails until he screams, "Jesus, Jesus save us all. Save us all Lord from the sins of the flesh. You know my heart, Lord. You know it!"

I am not the only one startled by his scream; my brother is no longer ignoring him. Mathew is crying. The tears are running down his Coca-Cola brown cheeks. My brother attempts to embrace him, but Mathew violently moves away, and once he starts moving he keeps moving down the row. He gets to the center aisle and briskly walks towards the Anderson's; my brother is steps behind him.

"Confess!" Mathew screams, "Confess to the Lord and to this congregation your adulteress sins. You harlot!"

He has drawn his arm back to strike, but my brother is there to coral him. Oh my God, it isn't Victor he is trying to attack; it's Victor's wife, Meredith. The deacons and some ushers have surrounded my brother and his husband, and they are roughly removing them from the sanctuary; too rough for my liking, so I stand and quickly follow. I catch up with them at the door leading to the back offices, meeting rooms, and Deacon's Hall. I grab the door just before it closes and locks. My mother is exiting from the pulpit door as Henry and myself enter the hallway. The deacons and ushers are moving like a security unit protecting the President. They enter through the double doors of Deacon's Hall as one. We: my mother, Henry, and to my shock, Mother York, are right behind them.

I think it's strange that Mathew isn't yelling and screaming considering seconds ago he was a rapid dog. When we all enter Deacon's Hall, no one is saying anything. The crowd of deacons disbands and leaves my brother and his husband standing in front of the long meeting table.

My brother and his husband are wearing matching brown suits and brown wingtip shoes. Jeremy is in finance, so the suit and shoes are appropriate for him; Mathew doesn't work, and to my knowledge hasn't worked since he was nineteen.

My mother clears her throat to speak, "What was happening out there?"

"Ask your son," Mathew snips while looking hard at Jeremy. Sweat is seeping from his forehead, and there is a little spittle on his lips, and a little snot hanging from his nose.

Some of deacons sit at the table and the others sit in the conference chairs surrounding it; my father remains standing at my mother's side. Mother York, who is standing next to my father says, "No, I think you should tell us, son. I heard what you yelled out in the sanctuary; relieve yourself, son."

Jeremy turns his whole body to face her, "Why are you here? This has absolutely nothing to do with you."

Mother York huffs, "As a church mother everything that happens in this church and to its congregation has something to do with me. I love this church and its members, so his outburst in our sanctuary "absolutely" has something to do with me, young man."
Shaking his head no, my brother says, "No, you are not here out of concern for this congregation; you are here being a nosey biddy."
"Jeremy!" My mother and father expel his name as if he were a child.

He turns from Mother York and reaches inside his suit coat and pulls out a handkerchief. "You need this," he says to Mathew and signals that he needs to clean his nose. Mathew grabs the handkerchief with no thanks.

After he wipes his nose, Mathew looks at my mother and says, "He has been sleeping with Dr. Anderson's wife; he is an adulterer."
"What?" My father and a couple of other deacons ask simultaneously. They look just as shocked as I am.

"Neither here or the church sanctuary is the place to discuss such private family matters; this is Easter Sunday, and we have a congregation waiting to praise the Lord. Jeremy and Mathew, I am going to ask you to wait here until after the service, or you are free to leave, and we can set up a session later, but I don't want you to return to the service this morning."

"You son-of-bitch!" is yelled from the doorway. Dr. Anderson is standing there trembling, "I trusted you man."

The deacons rise up from their seats.

"Whoa, no, no, no – this is not going to happen here and not like this." My mother directs with hands up in traffic guard fashion. "No, not like this . . . I will meet after service in my office . . . with both families."

"No, I don't see the need." Dr. Anderson says. "There is very little to talk about Pastor Jackson. My wife ran out of the church and left me and the children sitting in the pew; so the truth speaks for itself, my friend, my best friend fucked my wife." He deflates right in front of us all. He turns and walks away.

"You have to return to the pulpit," Mother York tells my mother. "I know," my mother snaps back. She takes a breath, "thank you." She takes another breath and leaves without saying another word. Everyone follows except Jeremy and Mathew.

While walking to our seats, I hear comments that surprise me: "There is always some mess when she comes," "Whatever happened, you best believe she was part of it," "What did she steal now," "Preachers kids are always the worst," "I know she ain't messing with a white boy," "You know she was on that stuff bad." When we sit, I think I imagined the comments until Henry grabs ahold of my hand and says, "Ignore ignorance. I love you, and you are the very strongest person I know."

It feels like eyes are boring through me, but when I look around
the congregation everyone is looking at my mother in the pulpit.
"Like our Lord, we rise from the death of sins. None of us are without sin, and none of us are finished sinning rather through omission
or commission. Let he who has not sinned throw the first stone.
"The good Lord knows the flesh is weak . . . he sent his son to help
us and forgive us because He knew. Lord, You know we are weak.
    Let he who has not sinned throw the first stone."
    "Preach!" Mother York shouts from behind us. "Preach it Pas-
tor!"
    Her shouts startle me and loosen my mind. Being in the church
has lulled my mind into remembrance and gave life to a part of me
that had been eradicated. I don't go to church. And I could care less
what people in a church think about me. It wasn't just the theft and
drug usage that kept away from the church. I stopped believing, not
in God, but in the church. I stopped believing in an outside interpre-
tation of God. God, my God is inside of me and I understand Her. I
came here to return the money I stole not to get pulled back into the
church. I exhale and smile. I lean over and kiss my blue-eyed boyfriend on the lips and say, "Thanks for coming with me."
    I reach into my purse and pull out the envelope filled with the
cash. I turn around in the pew and face Mother York, "Here is the
money I stole from the missionary found, will you make sure it gets
to the deacons and my mother." I drop the envelope in her lap not
waiting for a response. I stand and Henry stands with me. We both
exit with smiles on our faces. Whatever happens with my brother
and the Anderson's is church business, not mine. I will call my mother and father, and we will talk like we do most Sunday evenings.

I won't be calling my brother for a week or so letting the madness with his marriage settle down. I love this church, but attending it or any other church is in my past, and I will not allow it to weigh me down.

- Four -
The Cattle Call

Four heads, of which I am one, are bent over employment packets on the boardroom table. Our heads are in the third hour of what I nicknamed cattle calls. These cattle calls are open interviews for sales staffs, and none of the heads including myself enjoy them because of the low ratio of qualified applicants garnered form the calls. But the order came down from up high to do one, so we are doing one. Of the fifty-three packets already reviewed, the team has conducted a total of eight interviews with only one second interview extended.

I begin reading over my fifteenth packet of the morning, and I see the applicant has a Series 7 and 66 licenses, along with being a graduate of Michigan State and Kellogg, a TKE, and six years sales experience with Morgan Stanley.

The résumé causes me to pull up the chair's adjustment level bringing the heavily cushioned back straight. I pledged Tau Kappa Epsilon eight years ago myself. Looking to the papers on the table, I find the résumé's accompanying application and check the referenc es; none of the five names ring a bell.

"Hey Reynolds, it's time for a smoke break." The sandpaper scratchy voice of Patrick Kearny, a constant irritant to me, and the firm's most productive sales manager, interrupts my reviewing of the employment packet.

My eyes remain on the résumé not looking up at Kearny because I don't want to see his cherub round face grinning and trying to promote an "ok go smoke" out of me. Smoking is a weakness. A horrible habit I kicked six years ago because it represents a character flaw. A person that smokes knowing that smoking is killing them is weak psychologically; there is no further explanation.

Not to mention that the disgusting addiction interferes with the work of the office, and of course it would be foul mouthed and disrespectful Kearny who requests the smoke break, and like mindless drones the other two team members will follow suit, and the employment interviews will come to a halt. Their three pairs of eyes are boring into the top of my head awaiting my response.

"Smoke if you must." Without looking up, I hear all three interviewers rolling back their chairs and leaving the boardroom.

"Nicotine junkies," I say once the door closes; there is no sense in insulting them outright. Sifting to the applicant's cover letter, I read that the he has been in the top five percent of producers for the past four years. The linen quality of résumé and cover letter impress me because I used the same paper during my job hunt. Although my hunt did not consist of cattle calls, I hand delivered three résumés: one to my uncle, another to the firm my brother started, and the third my father had me bring to Rufus - the Human Resources manager who retired when I graduated.

The applicant's undergrad transcripts show a 3.5 GPA with a solid 4.0 from the Kellogg MBA. This kid looks good on paper, sometimes the cattle calls pay off. The applicant really couldn't be a kid: four years of undergraduate work puts him at twenty-one, another two to three years at Kellogg had him at twenty-three or twenty-four, and six years at Morgan Stanley "the kid" was at least thirty, five years older than me.

I slip my feet back into the black wingtips preparing to go out to reception and call the applicant in for the first interview. Glancing again at the name atop the résumé, Vincent Murphy, that gives me pause. I look to the address, Southside . . . far south.

An ethnically mixed name from the Southside of Chicago could be a problem. But after three slow muttering cows, interviewing a stellar prospect would be refreshing. I twist my left foot, the larger one, down into my shoe and swing my feet from beneath the board-room table and bend down to my laces.

As the Human Resources manager, I am aware of the cultural climate of the firm, and before he retired and passed the job over to me, Rufus made it clear that the maintenance of the climate was the HR manager's responsibility. The senior partners of Reynolds, Coleman, and Baker are all white Anglo Saxon Protestant males; the next executive tier of management is close to the same with the exception being Patrick Kearny. Front line supervisors and the sales staff contain two women: one Mexican, one Iranian, and all were hired by me; doing what I can for diversity because this firm, like other financial services, will have to go global to survive, and being diverse is a must.

I was not thinking Human Resources when I graduated; the

monitoring of new laws, benefits package work, and staffing were the mundane tasks of clerks, not the duties of the top producing broker and the inevitable CEO of Reynolds, Coleman, and Baker that I am planning on becoming. The Global Marketing division with its world travel was for me, but my father, Todd Franklyn Reynolds II, wanted me in Human Resources, so HR it has been for the past four years. What I once thought of as a clerk's duties are the tasks that fill my days.

But, my patience has been rewarded. This morning my father laid a proposal on my desk for opening an office in Japan and asked me, "Do you think you can handle the Chef of Staff position? Baker's boy Chad will be Divisional Head, but you will be second in command."

"Without a doubt, Father," was my immediate response allowing a smile to break my usually serious face. I have worked on keeping the smiles to a minimal at the office; a focused demeanor works best here.

If the information concerning Japan had come from anyone else, I would have hugged them. The information moved me so, but my father and I don't hug. We never have. We are not a hugging family, but I do hug others . . . well no, I don't hug others either.

Before Todd Franklyn Reynolds II entered the corner of Human Resources, which I made into an office with partitions from the office supply catalogue, the pleasant odor of fresh Jasmine was in the air.

The owner of the building's flower shop, a small Filipino woman, whom I thought was Mexican, with large brown eyes dark enough to be mistaken for black pitched me on the elevator last spring about having fresh flowers delivered twice a week to the office. Agreeing to the deliveries proved a good decision because the fresh flowers do promote smiles, but the fresh scent of the Jasmine was bullied this morning. My father brought the pungent smell of sickness to my makeshift corner office. I think the bandage on his abscessing knee needed to be changed.

"Good," was my father's reply to me agreeing to accept the Chief of Staff position. He continued with, "because there were some concerns from the other partners, but I went to bat for you. The appointment is yours . . . and Son, I am certain this hasn't been an easy three years for you, but you have managed to keep your eyes and mind to the horizon."

Four years, but I didn't bother to correct him. I watched the slight jiggling of my father's jowls due to the Parkinson tremors, and I remembered my eighth grade tennis coach who introduced my father as a man among men at the Tennis Awards banquet. I was receiving a trophy for the most improved player, but my father, the keynote speaker, made no reference to my trophy. He only spoke of looking to the horizon and improving the future with hard work of the present. Would the tennis coach still think of my father with an abscessing knee and jiggling jowls as a man among men? I doubt it. Hearing my father going to bat for me against the other partners would have been a pleasure because most of the words that come through his whitened and capped teeth in regards to my brother or me are critical. My father's constant belittlement of our deeds as children and teens is what caused my brother, Todd, to open his own firm in lieu of working for the more established family one, "Father will stop a dandelion from growing, come work with me," my brother encouraged on my graduation day. But no, I followed my father's footsteps into Reynolds, Coleman, and Baker. However the payout, Japan with a leadership position, is close at hand.

Patrick Kearny and the rest of the sales staff could kiss my "daddy's boy" ass. As Chief of Staff of a division, my work, not the opinion of salesmen, will speak for me. The prejudiced judgmental thought of me somehow being lesser because I am a partner's son is over. Kearney and his salesman and all their snide and disrespectful comments proved to be fodder for my climb. The proposal has the office opening in three months, ninety days. That is a toilet flush away. Let the smokers smoke; I am Japan bound.

The Southside address under the name on the résumé almost causes me to stay seated, but the chance of a good interview motivates me to stand and walk down the hall toward reception. The pearl face of my Patek Philippe reads 10:30. My brother should be in his office by now. The second smile of the morning is expanding across my face; the conversation we will have about me going to Japan should be interesting. Todd will be both proud and a little envious.

The reception area and the applicant are steps away. Business requires the smile to leave my face. In the doorway behind the reception desk, I look into the waiting area and see about twenty remaining job seekers. Of the twenty, one is Black, and he is the only one looking in my direction with a smile. He is a weird looking guy with Asian eyes and straight Asian hair with dark brown regular Black guy skin.

He is sitting in the armchair that allows a visitor to see the entrance and the door leading to the bullpen and manager's offices.

The applicant's legs are crossed with a foot on his knee. He is wearing a blue Brooks Brothers suit. I am wearing the same suit in dark gray. He has on a crisp white shirt with a blue and gray striped tie, and black wingtips. He continues to look at me smiling.

"Vincent Murphy," I call, hoping it's not the arrogant Black guy. But of course, the Black man raises his hand, nods, and stands.

Damn it, the name and the address were indicators. This interview is going to be a waste of my time. Just once in seventy-five years has the firm of Reynolds, Coleman, and Baker hired a Black broker; Harold Washington was the mayor, and the office joke was that the broker didn't stay long enough for the ink on his business cards to dry. I might be able to hire Black woman, but a Black guy . . . the climate couldn't take it; people would be too uncomfortable; the arrogance Black males project doesn't add to the cohesiveness of a well ran firm.

"Come this way," I say not offering my hand when Vincent Murphy gets to me. I never shake the applicant's hand until after the first interview. There is no sense in extending false hope to jobseekers who might not be worth a moment's notice.

The boardroom where the interviews are held is large enough for semi-private interviews at the lengthy leather padded table. My suggestion of holding four interviews simultaneously works. It quickly eliminates the unqualified cows and unwanted job seekers such as Vincent Murphy.

The small reception area is deceptive to the true size of our firm; once an applicant walks through the door and down the short hallway, they see the broker's bullpen area, and the glass doors of the management offices that outline the bullpen. Never do I slow my pace when walking an applicant through. If they make it pass interview one then I give them tour.

When Vincent Murphy and I enter the boardroom, two of the interviewers are back from their smoke break; both are sales managers, Patrick Kearny and Troy Akron.

"Vincent Murphy meet Troy Akron and Patrick Kearny," I say. Troy Akron, a blond thirty year old who looks and at times acts like a nineteen year old walks directly to the applicant, "Vincent, man what's up? I didn't know you were looking. I thought Morgan Stanley had those platinum handcuffs on you, bro."

Troy Akron does extend his hand and shakes with Vincent Murphy, "You know we got something for you dudes this year during tournament, ain't gonna be another blow out. You can bet that, bro! We got that big kid from Chase running center dawg. No mo' blow outs."

I see Vincent Murphy's face relaxing with being recognized by Akron. He readily shakes his hand and smiles.

The urban dialect Akron chose to speak in causes my toes to ball up within my wingtips. Akron, a Princeton grad, is grating my nerves. I have never understood why white people think sounding like an uneducated Black person is cool. I am sure Vincent Murphy is offended . . . if I were Black guy, I would be.

"Wishful thinking Akron, if your squad had Lebron James and a young Larry Bird, you guys still wouldn't get the tournament trophy that steel is at home in our case." Vincent Murphy says to Akron.

"No, no, bro nothing is forever in that league, you know this." Bro, they are not brothers, and I have never heard Akron refer to anyone else as "bro." He must be stopped before Vincent Murphy justifiably goes postal.

"Ah, You two are acquainted, I see," I say interrupting.

"Yep, Me and Murph are in the same Thursday night Board of Trade league. The one I have been trying to get you to join for two years." Akron says and playfully punches me on the shoulder.
That was his first time touching me in the four years I have been at the firm, and I don't plan on it happening again anytime soon; I step out of Akron's reach.

I detest basketball because people assume since I am 6'3" that I can play the game. I can't play. My father didn't allow my brother or me to play as children; calling it "a coon's game" and he insisted that we both played tennis and golf.

"Murphy's team won the league's finals two years in a row, and he got MVP both years, but times are changing, bro. We are bringing the thunder this year," Akron says answering my question, but patting Vincent Murphy on the back.

"Thunder without lighting is all noise Akron, and that's all I am hearing from you now, noise." Vincent Murphy adjusts his tie at the knot, "history speaks for itself."

"Murphy," Patrick Kearny stands from the table extending his hand as well.

Vincent Murphy shakes it and answers, "Kearny."

"The links Sunday?" Kearny asks.

"Wouldn't miss it for the world."

"Bring your money."

"I won't need mine if you're coming." Vincent Murphy beams a smile.

"You needed it last week."

" That was fluke Kearny, and we both know it."

"Whatever Murphy, your five C-notes comforted me all the way home."

I pray my mouth isn't hanging open. Several times Kearny has been called to carpet due to me reporting his inappropriate comments about Blacks during staff meetings, and each time my father squashed the complaint offering excuses such as, "Boys will be boys," or "Those are colloquialisms, don't take him serious."

A man who has made as many hateful statements as Kearny has about Blacks shouldn't have Black friends or social acquaintances. Being unable to stop myself from asking the obvious I say, "You two are acquitted as well?"

With a toothy grin Kearny answers, "Murphy is the newest member of my country club, and luckily he was placed in my tee off party. Well, lucky at least for me because his golf game is about as good as yours, Calvin."

That was a shock. I would have bet my Bimmer that Kearny didn't play golf with a Black guy.

"Calvin, I need the keys out of your office. Can I get them before you begin interviewing Murphy," Kearny walks for the door.

There are no keys in my office for Kearny; the only things in my office associated Kearny is the pack of cigarettes and a lighter that I took off the bathroom sink while he was in a stall smoking despite the city ordinance and my memo, but Kearny doesn't know I have the cigarettes. He came out the bathroom accusing others of stealing them. I am hesitant to leave the boardroom, but I figure Kearny asking for the keys is a roust to speak to me outside of the boardroom.

When I walk out, Kearny closes the boardroom door and pulls me by my suit jacket towards the bullpen stopping at the first sales desk. I have to forcibly wipe his hand from my jacket, "Have you lost your mind?"

Kearny rolls his eyes to the top of his head and ignores the question, "Listen to me Daddy's Boy,"

Through instantly tighten lips and clenched teeth I say, "I've told you about calling me that."

I am aware that "Daddy's Boy" is what every sales person in the firm calls me behind my back, but Kearny is the only one bold enough to call me the name to my face.

Kearny takes in a deep breath and makes an audible sigh exhaling, "Ok . . . Calvin . . . listen to me . . . that guy there," he hikes his thumb back towards the boardroom, "is Black Chicago wealth. His personal book of business includes Jordan, Oprah, Kanye, Jessie, and any other spook you can name in Chicago with money."

Again my lips tighten, "No racial epithets please, you know better, Kearny."

Dismissing my compliant with a nit clearing wave, Kearny runs his hand over the crown of his bald head and gets close enough for me to smell his breath mint and cigarette and see the sun burned skin crusted atop his nostrils, "Hear this Daddy's Boy, if you let that Black person walk out of here without making him an offer, I will personally shove my whole foot up your ass. I don't know why he is looking for a new job, but whatever the reason lock him in. Give him whatever the fuck he wants. I'm going to pull Akron's dumb ass out of there, and you go back in and close him like your balls depend on it because they do. I am going to send in your daddy in about ten minutes, don't fuck it up. That guy in there is flown to DC once a month to play basketball with Obama. He is not your run of the mill BET Black guy. Handle it the right way Calvin."

There is heat at the nape my neck, which is always present when talking to Kearny, but this time the warmth is spreading and moving up to my cheeks. I must be turning red. Kearny is a small minded antiquated 1950's throw back, I know that, but knowing doesn't stop me from reacting to his callousness.

The smart thing to do in this situation is to smile and nod which is what I do, "Thanks for the advice. I will do my best."
As long as Kearny is the number one producer, I have learned he is as much a part of the firm as a partner, and any intervention on my part is pointless

"You do that, Daddy's Boy." Kearny pokes me in the chest with his index finger, turns, and walks back to the boardroom.
My mind and eyes are on the pressure and smudge Kearny's poke left in my flesh and on my tie.

"You fat, stubby, baldheaded, son-of-a-bitch if you ever touch me again I will have your job."

None of the employees passing hear my heated words. I exhale, adjusts my tie, run my hand down my jacket, and walk back to the boardroom. When I get to the door Kearny, Akron, and the HR generalist are exiting.

"Good luck," Akron quietly says in passing.
I enter and close the boardroom door behind myself. Vincent Murphy is still standing next to the table with attaché case in hand.
"Please have a seat, Mr. Murphy."

"Vincent, please," he says pulling out the chair closest to him but not sitting.

I am aware that he is waiting for me to sit first. I do and position his résumé in front myself on the table. Vincent sits across from me.

"Six years with Morgan Stanley, wow, why are you looking?" When I shift my attention from the résumé to Vincent, I can't read the expression on his face. A smile of sorts, but his brown eyes have a serious cast. He looks as if he is questioning something.

"A number of reasons, Mr. Reynolds," a pregnant pause follows, but I don't give the permission for my first name to be used. I see Vincent's eyebrows raise and fall in a millisecond.

"The most important reason being upward mobility. I don't see a clear career path to management in my division. The management above me is five to ten years my senior. Advancement will come only if one them leaves, and that doesn't appear to happening any time soon."

I nod in agreement, "Understandable. Well, we are growing as I'm sure you are aware."

Vincent is not really smiling, but I see his teeth. I make a mental to practice such a look in the mirror; it has quite a disarming effect.

"Yes, the word on the street is Japan, and as my résumé reflects I speak Japanese fluently and spent twelve years there as a child and into my teenage years. My father was career military, and my mother is Japanese; so I, we, visit frequently. I have travel plans at the end of this month. A vacation to Tokyo with my fiancée; she has never been."

I must have heard him wrong. My eyes are fluttering, damn it. How could he possibly know of Japan? The proposal was dated with today's date. My blinking has stopped thank God. I was just told this morning. Why would a job applicant be aware of it?

"You've heard of our possible expansion to Japan?"

" Yes, I had an early breakfast with a recruiter this morning who was fishing the idea. I figured if she was fishing . . . I would go straight to the source."

"Which recruiter?" "The girl from Banner, Beatrice."

Beatrice is Chad's sister. He and three other people make up the Global Marketing arm of our firm. It makes sense for him to head the division in Japan. The plan may have just been mentioned to me, but obviously others have been working on it. No matter, last man on the deal team to know or not, Japan is in my future.

"And Beatrice was searching for management?"

"No, her interest seemed to be sales staff, and that was another reason I answered your employment advertisement. I figured if I came in it would improve my chances for management consideration."

"Understandable, but at this juncture we are only interviewing for sales staff for this office, the Chicago office. Would you be interested? And please keep in mind that we do offer an excellent management training program."

"What would be the time-line for consideration for Japan?"

"There is no concrete time-lime. It would depend on your personal development which will overseen by a sales manager."

"Oh, I see."

I see disappointment in Vincent Murphy's expression and hear it in his voice and for some reason . . . I am pleased by it.

The boardroom door opens and Vincent and I look to it and see my father entering.

"You know . . . it is the darnedest thing. I had just got off the phone with Beatrice about a Vincent Murphy, and then Kearny comes into my office telling me that there is an outstanding candidate interviewing in the boardroom named Vincent Murphy. Are the two the same sir?" my father asks Vincent.

"Yes, Mr. Reynolds," he answers standing and extending his hand.

My father shakes his hand and smiles, "And you know something else, I got a call from Jackson Murphy this morning. We both sit on the YMCA and Culture Center boards. He called me about his son interviewing with my firm. Boy, you pulled out all the stops didn't you?" My father is still shaking Vincent Murphy's hand and still smiling.

"Yes sir, I did."

"That's good, real good to see." My father lets go of Murphy's hand and sits next to me. Vincent also returns to his chair.

"Well, from what your dad tells me you have been looking for an opportunity to work in Japan?"

"Yes sir, I have."

"And he says you speak Japanese as well as your mother."

"Not quite sir, but I do speak it a tad better than my father."

"Well, that is a strong plus for you here, and Kearney tells me you have a book of business consisting of some of the city's most prominent citizens. We could certainly use that with opening a foreign office. Do you think you clients would have an interest in the Asian market?"

"Yes sir, and those that don't will have once I layout the perspectives for them."

"Good, good, well, I see no reason why not to welcome you to Reynolds, Coleman, and Baker."

What? No. I must not have heard him right. I am look steadily at my father hoping to catch his glance, so he can see the disapproval in my expression, but our eyes don't meet. Who does see my expression is Vincent Murphy, and he slightly shakes his head to the negative in response to it.

"Go on back to Morgan Stanley and do what you have to do wrap things up, but don't take more than three weeks. We want you involved with the Japan move. Beatrice told me your sales numbers and they're fantastic. You will be reporting directly to my son as a broker. Preliminary plans have a staff of fifteen brokers, but everyone going over is expected to sell."

What is my father doing? Only family is hired on a handshake at Reynolds, Coleman, and Baker. My father is smiling as if he has just been given a new knee or something, He rises from the chair and to me he says, "A fifteen percent increase to the package he had at Morgan Stanley, and we will cover all of his relocation expenses. Again, welcome aboard Vincent, and you and your parents have to come out to the house soon for dinner. No is not an option." He winks at Vincent.

"Mr. Reynolds, I am more than flattered by your offer, but unfortunately . . . I cannot accept. I do not believe me and," he opens his palm toward me "this Mr. Reynolds will work well together as subordinate and superior. I am uncertain as to why but there is some hostility between us."

"You two had relationship before today?" My father asks.

"No," we both answer.

What hostility? I have been as professional as possible with him. He must be one of those over sensitive Black guys who think everyone white is a racist. He is looking at my father and purposely not making eye contact with me. My father looks from him to me back to him and again to me with a questioning look that I can't answer, so I decide to ask Vincent Murphy what is he talking about.

"Vincent, what hostility are you speaking of?"

His eyebrows rise, "Are you kidding?"

"No, not at all." I say.

"Ok, first you refused to shake my hand when we met, and then you walked so fast in hall that I had to almost jog to keep up with you. It was as if you were trying to get the interview process over as quickly as possible. If Akron and Kearney weren't there, I would not have interviewed. I would have left and never... My father interrupts with a chuckle, "Ok, now I understand, Vincent. Please allow me to explain, my son is a very focused person. He is often mistaken for being rude, and he does take a little getting used to . . . with that being said . . . perhaps this will be best, we here at Reynolds, Coleman, and Baker are willing to offer you the Sales Manager's position. As the Sales Manager, you and Calvin would be equals both reporting to Chad. How does that sound?"

What the fuck just happened?

"Yes, as equals I think we could work together," Vincent agrees.

No, we could not work together because we are not equals; I have been at this firm for four years. I have a vested interest. My grandfather founded the firm. Vincent Murphy just walked through the damn door, and we are equals? The sickness in my father's knee must have spread to his brain.

"Good, very good then Sales Manager it is." My father smiles and winks again at Murphy. He stands and so does Murphy, and they shake hands across the table. I stand and extend my hand, and Murphy gives me a firm handshake along with his teeth-bearing look. Every muscle in my face is resisting, but I get the smile out while shaking his hand, "Welcome aboard."

"Well, I am going to leave you two to it. I have some calls to make." My father makes his exit leaving the boardroom door open. "What a great guy, it had to be wonderful having such a powerhouse for a father? Shall we move through the paper work now or later?" He asks still showing his teeth but not smiling.

Never is what I want to say to his smug ass, but what I say is,

"Later, after the offer letter is drawn up . . . and again, welcome. I will contact you this afternoon and set up the time."

Vincent steps away from the table with attaché case in hand as both Kearny and Akron enter the boardroom.

"We heard from the boss, welcome bro, Japan! That means you won't be playing in the Chicago league see ya!" Akron is joyous. Both he and Kearney are patting Vincent on the back.

The three have huddled together at the head of table. I exit and head to my makeshift office. The walls of the hall seem to be moving past me, and it feels like I am walking up hill. Stopping at the water fountain, I actually have to grab the chrome sides to balance myself. I bend to drink and water splashes on Murphy's packet, but the good paper holds the ink, and the print doesn't run.

At my desk, the scent of fresh Jasmine has returned. I sit and breathe it in. Equals . . . not in this lifetime, while putting Murphy's packet in my desk drawer the cigarettes and lighter taken from

Kearney catch my eye. Why not?

I tap a cowboy killer from the pack and flip the top of the Zippo and spin the wheel. The fire dances forth on the first attempt. The cigarette is in the flame and I inhale. With a flip of my wrist, I snap the Zippo closed. Leaning back in my chair I blow a cloud that lingers over my desk. I inhale and blow another. I put the cigarette out on the corner of my cheap desk and pick the phone up and dial my brother's number.

"Todd Reynolds," he answers on the second ring.

"Is the offer still on the table to work with you?"

"Always Calvin, full partner when you walk through the door."

"I am on my way."

There is nothing I need to take from my desk, but I do pick up the Jasmine plant, the lighter, and the smokes.

- FIVE -
A SUNNY DAY IN THE PARK

What he is demanding of me will destroy my soul. I will become like him – a dead man walking. My thought was that this one bad deed would correct my horrible mistake. I now see that the thought was wrong, murderously wrong.

There was supposed to be money here, a lot of money, but we have found none. We did find drugs; the wrong drug as far as I am concerned. Heroin is what The Walking Dead needs, so he is satisfied and anxious to leave, but I need to correct my blunder. Lord, I wish it wasn't so hot in this tin box.

The daughter swears cash is coming. The Walking Dead wants me to shoot her in the head and leave. He believes there is enough heroin to make us both rich. He is a heroin addict. A monkey cannot sell bananas as far as I am concerned, and my knowledge of drug distribution would not fill a roach sack. His plan is foolish, but he does have a point about the daughter. If we leave her alive, she will without-a-doubt tell her father we robbed his trailer. The daughter is on her knees pleading for her life. My pistol is at the back of her head. Her stringy blond hair is clumped with perspiration. Her hair is the same shade of blond as my wife's, and both of them are in need of a good shampoo. Last month, I started shampooing heads at Florien's. She pays me ten dollars a head plus tips. It's not bad money, but crack cocaine takes it right away. The money is gone before we can do anything with it. My wife and I are both strung out on crack.

No one was to be in this trailer. Everybody in the park knows whose trailer it is and what he uses it for. Nobody has been stupid enough to attract her father's raft especially after he set poor Jacob and his wife afire. It was only by the grace of God that their little boy child got out of the blazing trailer alive. If I leave the daughter alive, I am killing my wife and myself. But I am not a murderer. Pulling this trigger is not in me.

While wiping the sweat from my eyes with my forearm, the pistol accidentally nudges her head. She pleads again, "A lot of money is coming; that's the God's honest truth. I was waiting for Daddy to make the drop, and then I was going to take the money. You know I have the combination. The money is coming. I swear."

Her plan is for the three of us to leave and come back after her father makes the drop. According to her, the drop will be over a hundred thousand dollars. That was what The Walking Dead and I expected to find in the safe. He got the heroin because the daughter was too scared to lie about the safe combination. She's begging for her life, so I doubt that she is lying about the money either.

The problem with her plan is where to go after we walk out of here. My trailer is five lots down, and The Walking Dead lives on the other side of the park. If anyone sees the three of us together, it's bound to cause talk: the owner's bratty nineteen year old daughter with The Walking Dead and me - the half Black - half white stud lesbian of the park.

"It's her life or ours, Aggie. Shoot the little cunt," comes from the mouth of The Walking Dead. With the briefcase of heroin under his arm, his dope fiend mind is on getting out of here fast. He is standing at the trailer's front door peeping out of the half window into the bright light of the afternoon. It's scorching outside. It's been blazing for a month, no rain, just dry hot heat from a mighty ornery sun.

"If you can't do it, toss me the pistol and I'll shoot her."
He turns from the half window to face us. If I did toss him the pistol, he couldn't catch it with the briefcase under his arm and the butane torch tank in his other hand. I should throw it to him and watch him try to juggle all three items.

The Walking Dead, Milton, is dressed in a pair of blue jean cut offs that he has worn the whole summer. The shorts expose his frog legs and blue and green varicose veins, his knobby knees, and cruddy caved in ankles. His grimy callused feet are in dollar store clear plastic flip flops, and a filthy red and yellow stained long sleeve gray thermal t-shirt covers his upper torso.

People who don't mind their hygiene irritate me. Milton infuriates me with his twice a year bathing . . . at least that's how he smells. If it wasn't for my recent addiction and my current need, I would never be in his disgusting company. This pistol is getting heavy, and the daughter's continuous crying is trying. If I don't kill her, I'm dead. If I do kill her, my soul is damned. My mama used to tell me the only thing a person has of eternal value is their soul. And life is a test of how clean you can keep it. Sins and bad deeds stain the soul. God . . . how did I end up here?

I don't need a deity for the answer. I am here because of crack cocaine and that nasty fool at the door.

"It's enough money for all of us," the daughter pleads from her knees. "All I want is enough to leave town and start over. I have a new beginning waiting for me in Seattle, Aggie. Either Daddy, or this life will find me up there . . . please . . . we can all get what we want. You don't have to kill me. I want to live. I want a life, a real life like everybody else, but I will never have that here. In this town, in this state, I will always be Jerry Mac's daughter, nothing more. The only life I will have is the one he thinks his daughter should have. I deserve more. Leaving is the only way for me to have my own life, and that money is my ticket out."

She has turned her head and scooted around on her knees to face me. Looking into her face, I lower the pistol. She has nerve. I couldn't have moved with a pistol to my head.

"Please, it's enough money to share."
For all her crying, one would think her eyes would be puffy and red. They're not. If not for hearing her cry, I wouldn't think the girl had shed a tear. The whites of her blue eyes don't show a trace of the distress her sobs owned.

"Where can we go?" I ask her. "People in the park can't see us together. I'm not moving to Seattle after this is done. I still have to live here."

Milton abruptly walks from the front door to us. He draws the briefcase over his shoulder and swings it down striking the daughter across her face. The corner of the case hits her like a fist and sprawls her out on the gritty ivory tile. She's not out cold, but he dazed her good. Her head is about a foot away from the only thing in the trailer not attached to the wall, the safe.

The daughter whimpers and he stomps her stomach. I move to him and put the pistol to his forehead. I brought this pistol last year to shoot on New Year's Eve, so people in the park would know me and my wife had protection. I figured if they heard me shooting they would know I had a gun, and so far no one has tried to break in on us. The hammer on the pistol pulls back a lot easier than the trigger.

"Get off her." My teeth are clenched tight. I feel blood rushing through my temples. She didn't deserve to be struck like a dog especially by the likes of him. The pistol with cocked hammer has bucked his jaundice eyes.

God please help me because none of the hesitation that was present when I had my pistol to the girl's head is here now. I want to pull the trigger and blow a hole clear through the leather of his forehead and the back of his greasy head. It's his fault that I am here. It was him who brought up the idea of stealing the money in the first place. He said it would be "a walk in the park."

My wife told him about my need, and once he had that information, he wouldn't let up. He has been constantly running the plan into my head. If I was sitting on the trailer steps, he was whispering it in my ear. When my wife and me sent him to get crack, as soon as he got back he would start talking about the plan. He had so much information on her Jerry Mac's schedule and doings that eventually his continuous conversation about robbing the trailer seemed practical. He didn't plant an acorn; he planted the whole oak in my mind. This situation is his fault.

"Don't shoot him," comes from the floor. "The noise will draw attention."

His yellow orbs are rolled up and focused on the barrel of the pistol that I am boring into his head, "She's in our way, Aggie. We don't need the money she's talking about. We can get all we need with this H."

The air around him is fetid with feces and vomit. I want out of his putrid company. The idea hits me as hard as his odor.

"Take the freaking case and leave. The heroin is yours. We will stay for the money."

"What?" His eyelids are fluttering. He looks from the gun barrel to me then back to the barrel then to me again. "Are you saying I can leave?"

Everyone in this trailer is dripping sweat, but his is offensive. "You heard me. Leave." I poke him harder in the head with the pistol. The intensity of the poke causes him to make an immediate turn from me and exit. It's not until I hear the screen door close do I lower my pistol.

Leaning on the kitchen counter, I am helping the daughter from the floor.

"You wanted to shoot him, didn't you? That wasn't smart letting him leave here with the drugs. Daddy want leave the money when he sees the heroin is gone. You weren't thinking, Aggie."

At this point, all I want to do is go home and kiss my wife and think up an alternative plan for coming up with the money. Ten years ago, I graduated number three from my high school class, and I almost finished college. I stopped my studies when my mother became ill. I am all she has. A brain tumor took my father when I was twelve.

"You're right. It wasn't smart, but it ended it and no one got murdered."

I should be able to come up with a non-violent solution to this money problem. Smoking crack and being in Milton's company has me thinking like a criminal. My plan won't involve a gun or robbing anyone.

"But I am stuck here with no way out, and staying here is a death sentence for me, a slow death, but still a death. I won't stay here. Whatever it takes, I am getting out." The daughter says.

The mark above her eye will turn purple and make a knot. She's unsteady but standing. I brought my wife the same pink sundress the daughter is wearing. However, my wife would not be caught dead wearing hers without four-inch heels. The daughter has on matching pink slide in sandals. Leaning on me for balance she says, "We should leave too. Daddy will be here any minute. He never misses the lunch my mother brings him."

I have no destination in mind, but we are moving towards the door until we see The Walking Dead backing up through the door with both hands up. Milton has no briefcase or torch. Once he enters, he continues to back up. We stop. The case and torch are flung into the trailer and land at Milton's elephant skin feet. A white shoe and white pant leg are seen at the break of the door. I know who it is, and so does the daughter; her breaths become rapid.

"It's Daddy," she whispers.

When her father enters, a breeze accompanies him, not a cool breeze but a warm burst. It moves through the whole trailer with his glance. When his eyes get to his daughter and me, he releases an audible grimace.

"What are doing in here Jeanette, and what happened to your face?"

Dressed in white linen pants and a white short sleeve shirt, one would think a cool breeze would have blown in with him. He is the only one in the trailer not sweating. His arms are hanging loosely at his sides in his right hand is a silver gun with a black tip. It doesn't have a cylinder in the middle like mine, and his is longer even without the black thing on the end.

"I asked what are you doing in here, and what happened to your face?" He snarls.

The daughter stops leaning on me. Matter of fact she stands up straight and walks effortlessly over to her father. He is only a couple inches taller than her about five eight, my height. The walking dead is the tallest person in the trailer. He is over six feet even with his hunched back. His arms are still in the air.

"I was walking past the trailer Daddy and saw the two of them in here. I came in to see what was going on, and that guy hit me with a torch. He was trying to break into your save but couldn't. He threatened to kill me because he didn't want me to tell you. I opened the safe for him to save my life. He was still going to kill me, but Aggie stopped him. She saved my life, Daddy.

Before me or Milton can say a word in dispute, the loosely hanging arm with the big silver pistol raises and three zip, zip, zip sounds are heard. The first two zips caused Milton to take two steps back. The last zip rocked his head back and toppled him over.

I want to raise my gun purely as a defensive move, but no part of my body feels capable of motion. He shot Milton down. Pouring sweat and free flowing urine appears to be all the motion I am capable of. The desire to swallow is strong, and my pistol should be raised. I should say something in protest before he shoots me down as well.

Without concern, he takes steps to where Milton's carcass lays. He steps over it to pick up the briefcase and walks over to the safe. He rolls the numbers, opens it and places the case and a large manila envelope from under his shirt within the safe. He closes the black steal door.

Without turning from the safe he says, "Thank you for saving my daughter's life. That is the only reason I am not going to shoot you in your lesbian brain because there is no reason in the world for you to be in my trailer, unless you came to rob me too. And drop that pistol before I change my mind and put a hole in your head."
I drop my gun, "Sir I didn't . . ."

Looking at the safe and not at me he says, "Don't say a word, not one. I need to think. Leaving you alive could cause me problems. And you know something? You have been a problem since before you were born. It all started when your Black ass daddy got your mama pregnant and moved into the park with her. He was the first black man to live in this park. A lot of people wanted to burn them out . . . You know I could have been your daddy, but your mama loved that Black boxer. He never did earn more than beer and rent money from fighting, but she stayed with him. So now she has you . . . you."

He turns from the safe to me, but he doesn't really look at me. He's looking past me. "You pissed your pants not so tough after all, huh?"

Tough, what gave him that impression? I know why. It's because I take care of my wife and myself and don't ask any man for help. That makes men think I am trying to be tough. I am not tough or hard. I merely take care of me and mine.

"You took a second mortgage on your mother's trailer, didn't you?"

To my shame, I did.

"Sir?" now it's me not looking at him.

"Look you he/she or she/he don't make me repeat myself."

The daughter stomps her foot on the trailer floor and gets her father's attention. "Daddy, why are you talking to Aggie like that? She helped me."

He pushes her aside and squeezes off three more zips from his pistol that land between my feet. I involuntarily drop to my knees, and my right knee lands atop my pistol.

To the daughter, he says, "Never go against my actions. If I so desire, I will take this freaks life."

And he sounds like he will. I look up at her not him. She doesn't flinch. She calmly says, "Please don't hurt her. Aggie is my friend." This is news to me. I can count the times on one hand when we have spoken to each other. I need to get off of the floor and out of this trailer.

Her father steps away from her and closer to me, "Since when do you have a lesbian friend, especially one that steals from her own mother?"

If I tried to get up now, I couldn't, not without touching him. He's talking to her but looking hard at me. I put a second mortgage on my mother's trailer. The crack cocaine had me take the loan three months ago without her knowledge. After her stroke a year ago, she gave me power of attorney over her affairs. I can sign my name for hers. We did this to help her, but once I started smoking crack, helping her was not foremost in my mind getting more crack was. Over the three months, my wife and me smoked up the twenty five thousand dollar loan and couldn't make the first payment. The trailer my wife and I live in is a rental. My mother owned hers free and clear. It is all she has from thirty years of being a waitress, and I mortgaged it away.

The father runs his clear day blue eyes all over me as if he's summing me up and coming up with zero. His attention goes to his daughter, but only for a moment. He looks at Milton and pulls a phone from his pocket and dials a number, "Teddy, I got garbage at the safe house. It needs immediate disposal."

He clicks the phone off and turns back to me, "I am assuming you being in my trailer with that scum," he points to Milton's body with his pistol, "has to do with your inability to pay back the second mortgage."

He is silent. Giving me an opportunity to answer, but I can't.

"Yeah, I thought as much. This is what I am going to do. You come by my office at ten in the morning . . . and be on time, and for saving my daughter's life, and for your mama's good, and your silence concerning this situation . . . I will settle the mortgage loan for you, but you are in my debt. You owe me."
I want to kiss his feet.

"Oh, and wear a dress to my office. How you dress disturbs my wife."

To get a fix for the second mortgage, yes, I will take off my khakis and white t-shirt and put on a dress. I want to ask about the debt, but I don't. He will probably have me laboring around the park. I stop myself from asking him is he sure. What I know of him stops me. He is a man that does what he says. I watch him walk to his daughter,

"Let's go, Jeanette."

"No, I'm going to stay here a minute with Aggie. I'll meet you at the office."

"What is it with you and her?" When he says 'her,' he points the long pistol at me. "Has she done something to you?"

He looks down at me like he just caught me pulling my tongue from her mouth.

"If you have touched my daughter . . ." spittle spews from his mouth.

"Nothing happened between us Daddy that I didn't want to happen."

Oh Lord, what is she saying?

I hear the zips and see pieces of the tile flying up all around me. I pull my gun from under my knee and pull the trigger as many times as I can. Spots on my body, mostly in my chest, are on fire. I see red splatter across the father's face, and he topples back like Milton. He's motionless on the floor. I have to lie down. I go from knees to my stomach. The spit that comes from my mouth is red. I want to go home and be with my wife.

Rolling over I see the daughter at the safe. She retrieves the envelope and the briefcase. She bends down to get the butane torch. I aim my gun at her and pull the trigger, no more bullets. She turns the torch on full blast and places it on the end of the counter above me. She blows out the pilots on the stove and turns all the knobs to high. The daughter hurriedly goes to her father and picks up the long gun. She stands over me. I see her pink sandals.

Dear Lord, who will take care of my wife and mother, "Don't please."

It is not words she answers with; I hear only zips.

- Six -
A Smart Kid

When Mr. Pratt called his name last week, Walter thought it was a mistake. At best he had been a C level student. All the names Mr. Pratt called, besides his, were Honor Roll students: the A, B students, or the smart kids. Walter Smith had never thought of himself as smart, a quick learner yes but not particularly smart.

Smart kids were different than him. They got As all the time, they spoke well, they enjoyed doing homework. This trip, this competition, was for the smart kids. But somehow he was on the short bus with them going to represent The West Side Academy in the state's History Bowl finals. His area was to be African American History. Mr. Pratt told him that without a doubt he was the student body expert on African American History.

Initially, Walter thought Mr. Pratt was making a racist joke calling him "the student body expert on African American History" because he was one of The West Side Academy's ten African American students. But, he soon saw that the statement wasn't a snipe at him, but a need for the school. During last year's competition, the only area where the school fell short was in African American History. Had there been a student in possession of a minute portion of the history, the school would have fared better and possibly won the Bowl. They lost last year's competition by fourteen points. The African American history questions totaled twenty points; of that twenty, the West Side Academy received none.

Walter didn't think his knowledge of African American History was that extensive. He knew the few facts his papa insisted he know, and the stuff he looked up because of the facts. When his papa told him that other Black Muslims murdered Malcolm X in 1965, he did an internet search and learned about Malcolm's birth place, his parents, Elijah Muhammad, and the Black Muslim movement.

While in American History class with Mr. Pratt, Walter pointed out that the book they were studying from erroneously listed Malcolm X's date of birth as 5-19-35. When he pointed out the error, Mr. Pratt argued that perhaps he was wrong and the book was right. The next day Walter brought in a full report on Malcolm X with the correct birth date of 5-19-25. The report, along with the three different sources he found for Malcolm X's correct birth date brought him to Mr. Pratt's attention.

For Walter, looking up information about Black people was fun. It was just like finding out about Mixed Martial Arts fighters, or cars with V8 engines and big blocks, or throwback gym shoes. Finding out about stuff didn't make him smart at least not in his opinion. That evening after boarding the bus to the competition, Walter began to feel that he wasn't the only one doubting his academic abilities. The smart kids had all clumped together in the center of the short bus sitting next to each other, leaving him sitting alone behind

Mr. Pratt and a sleeping Coach Williams.

He didn't mind sitting alone because he could think of anything he and the smart kids would have to talk about. Walter was a Mixed Martial Arts fight fan. Jason, who Walter thought was the leader of the smart kids, said that caged martial arts bouts were all fake. Walter and Jason had two loud arguments about the sport's validity last week.

The first argument ended in the lunchroom when Jason informed those sitting at the table that only stupid people like trailer park white people and Black people believe that the "pseudo" sport was real. Walter wanted to go across the lunchroom table and show Jason just how stupid a young Black man could be, but he didn't. It was obvious that Jason was trying to goad him into a fight. Jason started the first argument the same day Mr. Pratt announced that Walter was going to the History Bowl.

The announcement was made over the school's P.A. system, and Walter was shocked to hear his name mentioned with Jason's and his bookworm crew. When he went to lunch, pink haired Mindy called him to the smart kids' table very excited, "Hey Walter, come eat with us!"

He would have ignored the call except for Mindy was ok with him; they had a history. She traded Pokémon cards with him in sixth grade, and she always gave him her pork entrees when she was served the non-kosher meat for lunch. Because of their history, he maneuvered through the crowded lunchroom to the smart kids' table.

He put his lunch tray on the end of the gray slate table next to Mindy's and sat in the empty space on the plastic bench next to her.

Mindy leaned over and hugged Walter and said, "I screamed when I heard your name! I told everybody here that you and I have been friends since kindergarten, and that we took naps together."

He returned the hug and the smile and remembered that they had napped together as kindergarteners.

They actually slept on the same mat because there was only one Big Bird mat, and they both wanted it. He had gotten to it first but to stop her from crying he shared it with her, and from there their kiddy age friendship sprouted, but now in high school they traveled in different circles and barely spoke to each other. She had her friends, and he had his.

That was why he was a little surprised by her sudden and open intimacy. After her initial hug and greeting, long seconds of uncomfortable silence passed at the lunch table. The lunchroom buzzed with kids, but the smart kids' table was silent. He watched Mindy looking into the other four faces at the table. He realized that it was only her who was excited about the announcement of him going to the competition, and it was only her who had extended the invitation for him to join them at their lunch table. The other four stoic faces refused to make eye contact with him.

Looking to break the ice, and to assist Mindy out of the blunder of the invitation he attempted a conversation.

"Did y'all see that Ultimate Warrior Challenge last night? Dude from Korea was off the chain!"

It was half a pineapple faced Jason who quickly answered with, "Only idiots with extremely low IQs watch that pseudo sport of buffoons."

"Huh?" Walter questioned.

"You heard me," Jason answered unsmiling.

Walter looked to Mindy who looked down at her lunch tray.

"So what... you don't like cage battles?" Walter asked Jason.

"No. I'm not a moron, so I don't enjoy broadcasts for the intellectually challenged."

Walter chuckled, shrugged his shoulders and said, "It's a sport dude, like boxing or kickboxing. Mixed Martial Arts is the next real thing. You should check it out." Walter lowered his eyes from Jason and picked non-existent lint from his yellow rugby shirt.

"It is as fake as Hollywood wrestling, and only trailer park white people and stupid Black people believe its authenticity."

Windy blew a throat deep breath and said, "Jason that isn't necessary," she pushed her tray to the center of the table, "it really isn't."

Jason pushed his tray across the table bumping Mindy's, "Yes, it is. He should be made aware of the caliber of people he will be traveling with. That is if he decides to attend the competition." Jason looked hard at Walter with challenge filling his gray eyes.

Walter returned Jason's hard stare. He was not surprised by what Jason said, but he was shocked by the openness of the statement. Usually racist kids say such things under their breath or while passing by in the hall. Overt racist statements were seldom heard in the school.

Forcing a smile on his face Walter said, "Dude, I was really thinking about not going. But now, you and a thousand other red necks couldn't stop me."

He thought about spitting on Jason's chicken sandwich, but he didn't want to risk suspension and not going to the competition.

"I'll talk to you later Mindy." Walter said standing with his tray. "Yes please depart. Perhaps cartoons are playing on the television monitor," was Jason's snide remark.

"Yo' mama," Walter said with the forced smile still plastered on his face. He turned and left without another word.

The second argument happened yesterday, and Walter started it in gym with the majority of the wrestling team present. The class had just dressed for gym and was exiting the locker room into the open gym area when Walter asked Jason, "Hey man, who did you say believes Mixed Martial Arts is real?"

Jason was at the front of the line filing into the gym. When he got into the gym he came into the presence of wrestling team practicing on the mats.

Walter yeld, "Jason, didn't you say only stupid people like Blacks and trailer park white people believe Mixed Martial Arts is real?"

Walter having wrestled his freshman and sophomore years knew the racial makeup of the team and the coaches: majority white, followed by Mexicans, and then Blacks. And he knew that all of them were Mixed Martial Arts fans. He expected his loud statement to get the attention of the gym, and it did.

"Didn't you say that Jason? Jason Wilson, didn't you say only stupid people like trailer park white people and Blacks believe Mixed Martial Arts is real?"

The students in line behind Jason faded away from the knock-kneed, rail thin Jason leaving him standing alone with a yelling Walter behind him and the wrestling team before him. The gym quieted with all eyes on Jason. Students were waiting for his answer.

The Black wrestling coach, Coach Williams, blew his whistle and yelled, "Drills!"

That command forced the gym into an uproar, which saved Jason from answering. Walter ran past Jason and hip checked him hard enough to send him tumbling to his buttocks. Walter and the others that had lined up for drill exercises laughed at Jason on the gym floor.

Jason stood, dusted himself off and gave them all the bird.

Nope, Walter didn't have much to say to Jason and his crowd. He settled down into the bus seat and pulled the blanket his mother insisted he take with him up around his neck. He looked out into the darkness made less by the city's streetlights and decided to join Coach Williams in sleeping.

He didn't feel as if he had slept long, but the sun was up and their bus was coming to a stop in a large group of buses in a Days Inn parking lot. Looking around he saw no neighborhood houses, stores, street light post, parked cars, or passing traffic. He saw only vast fields, one with little stubby green plants, and another with rows upon rows of green corn stalks. On the far horizon behind the Day's Inn, he saw a house with five fenced in horses.

Walter knew he was no longer in the city. The only street he saw was a highway, and the tallest structure he saw was a satellite tower. He knew it was going to be different down state, but he wasn't expecting the area to be almost empty of buildings.

Mr. Pratt stood from his bus seat cleared his throat and said, "Ok students, this is the list of roommates. It is non-negotiable, so save any grumbles and whines for your mommies and daddies when you get home. Ok, first we have Smith and Wilson..."

Walter heard no other room assignments after his and Jason's names were called. He looked toward the middle seats and saw Jason's mouth hanging open. By the disgruntle look on Jason's pimpled narrow face, Walter was certain he would complain to Mr. Pratt about the assignment. He decided to leave the protesting to Jason. If anyone is going to look like a complaining crybaby, he decided to let it be Jason.

Once off the bus with his bookless book bag on his shoulder, Walter was walking towards the doors of the Days Inn when pink haired Mindy swung her book bag into his. He noticed she was rolling a suitcase behind her.

"Hey Walter, I just wanted to apologized for what you went through in the lunchroom with Jason. We all don't feel as he does. Most kids are glad you are here."

He slowed down and blew his breath into his hand. He didn't want to talk to her with morning stank breath; he smelled no fouls odder in his palm. He allowed her to catch up and walk alongside of him.

"It's cool," he said, "it's only for two days and one night. I think I can handle the cold shoulder that long."

Mindy walked right alongside of him saying, "But that's what I'm trying to tell you, we don't want you to feel like we are all giving you the cold shoulder. You see Jason is a senior, and the Captain of the debate team, and the unofficial leader of the History Bowl team. Kids follow him even if we know we shouldn't. I should have said more that day at lunch, and I just want you to know that."

They paused at the double doors of the inn and Walter said, "Mindy we been cool since we were shorties that ain't gonna change because you got into a clique with a red neck, and besides most of my buddies don't like white people, but you still my girl." He opened and held a door for her allowing her to enter while pulling her suitcase through.

Inside the busy bright yellow and beige lobby she asked, "Really Walter? You have friends that don't like white people? Do they go to our school?"

Looking into her startled brown eyes he said, "Blacks are not excluded from prejudice thoughts Mindy."

Eyelids rapidly blinking she asked, "But you're not prejudice are you Walter? No, you're not. We've been friends a long time. I would know if you were prejudice. How silly I must sound. Forgive me please. Hey, where is your suitcase?"

"It's on my shoulder?"

"Then where are your books, journals, and notes?"

"I didn't bring any. What I know I know. What I don't, I don't."

Standing at the reception desk of the Days Inn's lobby pulling on a strand of her pink hair Mindy said, "That is a mighty cavalier attitude, mister. I could never be that confident." She smiled and adjusted her book bag on her shoulder.

Walter didn't view his lack of books and notes as confidence; stuff he liked he remembered, and he liked knowing stuff about Black people.

A group of girls passed them and Mindy said, "Well I going up to my room, see you later. Don't be late for the bus: 11:45 sharp. I always try to get there early just in case."

She rolled her suitcase by him to the elevators.

He watched her and the group of girls board the elevator, and he thought about her question.

Was he prejudice? Did he prejudge people based on their color? Did he expect white people to act a certain way just because they were white? He thought about Jason, and he remembered not being surprised by his statement at the lunch table, nor was he surprised by the displeased look on his face when he found out that they were roommates.

Walter wondered if his expecting Jason to be prejudice made him prejudice. Was he prejudging Jason by expecting him to be prejudice? Instead of boarding the elevator with the next group of students, he walked further into the lobby and sat on one of the empty flower patterned couches. His papa told him that prejudice people were closed minded people who learned very little.

When he looked toward the opening front doors, he saw Jason struggling through the doors with a laptop, two book bags, and a roller suitcase.

Forcing himself up from the couch, Walter rose and went to the doors to assist Jason. He held one of the double doors open and picked up one of Jason's book bags from the floor of the doorway.

"Are you still in 318 with me?" he asked.

"Yeah," was Jason's dry reply.

Walter hoisted Jason's book bag on his free shoulder and followed the group of boys to the elevator. He decided he was not going to prejudge Jason, and he was going to treat him with the golden rule Papa taught him: do unto others as you want them to do unto you.

In the bathroom of the room, all he pulled from his book bag was his deodorant, toothpaste, and toothbrush, which he placed on the sink. He went into the sleeping area of room and stretched out on the twin bed closest to the window while Jason unpacked his books. To Jason he said, "Hey, don't let me sleep past bus time, ok?"

Jason didn't answer.

"Did you hear me, man?" Walter asked.

"We are roommates. I am not you alarm clock. If you oversleep that is on you," Jason didn't look up and continued to unpack his books.

Maybe going back to sleep wasn't a good idea. Mindy did warn him not to be late for the bus. Walter picked up the television remote from the nightstand between the two twin beds and turned on the television. He began searching for B.E.T. When he fond the channel he was pleased because a video review show was on, and they were playing the top ten Rap videos.

"Yeah, this will keep me woke," he said out loud and turned the volume up on Lil' Wayne.

"Oh my God! Are you serious? Don't you want to review something?" was Jason's response to the increased volume of the television, "don't you need to check or verify some fact or date? Read something, or write something? Do something to prepare for the Bowl? Could you please turn it down?"

When Walter looked from the television to Jason, he saw his reddening cheeks and ears and his trebling lips and hands. It was obvious to Walter that Jason was truly upset. He turned the television off. "All you had to say was you needed to study man. I understand. You are not as ready as you would like to be, my bad. Go on and get you cram on. I'ma call down to the desk and get me an eleven o'clock wakeup call. Good luck with your cramming."

Walter picked up the phone from the nightstand and made the call. After, he rollled over to face the window and closed his eyes for a nap.

He heard, "Thank you," from Jason.

The competition was held in the town's high-school auditorium. The auditorium seats were filled, and people were standing along the back and sidewalls. Walter wasn't expecting a crowd, nor was he expecting to be on stage behind a podium. There are seven students on stage, and a moderator presenting the questions on an overhead screen. On each podium there was an electronic panel with the letters A, B, C, and D lit up.

They had been instructed by the moderator to push the letter that corresponded to their choice for an answer. They would be asked ten questions worth two points each. There were four schools represented on the stage, and each school had two student panelists. He alone represented The West Side Academy.

From the stage, he was able to spot Mindy, Mr. Pratt, and Coach Williams. He waved to Mindy, and she waved back smiling. All the students on stage and the moderator were Black. The moderator had black and grey locs and tortoise shell glasses. He cleared his throat and informed them again that only the first answer would be registered and tallied.

He began, "The first questions will center on Supreme Court decisions. In what year was the Dred Scott decision handed down?" Walter didn't hesitate: the answer was B - 1857. His papa had paid him ten dollars to find out about the man Dred Scott, the Black man who sued for his freedom, and while researching the man he found about the Supreme Court's decision. Walter was not only the first to answer but his is the only audience board that is lit. The other students didn't even attempt an answer.

"Correct. Student number three from the West Side Academy of Chicago. Two points to your credit."

Walter quickly winked at a smiling Mindy.

The moderator said, "Question number two: what practice among some of this Nation's public schools was overturned due to Brown v. Board of Education?"

Fast as greased lighting, as his papa would say, Walter pushed A for segregation.

"Correct, student number three."

Walter saw that all the other students answered, but he was first, and thereby he earned the points. He noticed Mr. Pratt and Coach Williams grinning from ear to ear in the audience.

The moderator looked in each student's face then he said, "The next two questions will center on African American first in sports. Who was the first African American Heavy Weight Champion of the World?"

Without hesitation Walter pressed D for Jack Johnson. Two students picked Joe Louis, two Joe Frazier, and the other two picked Muhammad Ali. Walter chuckled at their answers. From his papa telling him to find out about race riots in America, he learned about Jack Johnson and the race riots of 1910 that occurred because Johnson won the Championship.

The moderator smiled at Walter and said, "Congratulations student number three from The West Side Academy, your answer is correct."

Walter didn't want to look up at the scoreboard on the overhead, but he did, and he saw that only the West Side Academy had points. The moderator pushed his locs from his forehead and glasses and said, "The second question from the sport's history regarding African American first is from the arena of tennis. Who was the first African American woman to win the notable Grand Slam?"

Althea Gibson, he pressed B, but he did not get the points. "Congratulations student number one from Rockford. You answered correctly and first."

Walter looked to his left at student number one and saw a chubby round face on a large framed girl with her hair pressed and gleaming. Only he and she answered correctly, the others all picked either Venus or Serena Williams.

When Walter looked to the audience, he saw Mr. Pratt looking at the score board, Coach Williams was still grinning like he is at a wrestling match, and Mindy was moving down a seat making room for Jason.

The moderator cleared his thought and said, "We will continue with African American firsts; however, we will switch to literature. Question one: Who was the first African American to win a Pulitzer Prize?"

Walter pushed B for Gwendolyn Brooks with no hesitation and got the point. Out loud he said, "1950 for her book of poetry titled 'Anne Allen.'" He hunched his shoulders and added, "Being from Chicago you know, I gots to know that one," he flipped the collar of his white Polo button down and grinned. He looked over at the student who beat him on the Althea Gibson question and winked. She sucked her teeth at him and set her eyes straight ahead.

The moderator observed their exchange and chuckled, "Shall

we continue in the vein of awards in literature: Who was the first the African American to win a Noble . . ." before the moderator could complete his sentence Walter's nemesis pushed A for Toni Morrison. She got the credit and the points.

Walter laughed. The moderator nodded and said, "Congratulations student number one. Your answer is correct and first. Bully for you. That was a bold move indeed."

"Oh it's on now," Walter said.

"It has been on. I thought you knew," were the muffled words from his challenger.

When he looked to her, he saw her eyes set forward on the overhead screen.

The moderator said, "I think you young scholars will appreciate this next category. We continue with first. No, allow me to clarify, not first but the oldest. The subject matter is Historically Black Colleges and Universities. Which is the oldest Historically Black College or University, or HBCU in America?"

With little interest in going to college since college is for smart kids, Walter had done no research with regard to HBCUs, and he didn't have a clue to the answer.

His nemesis however did. She answered A for Cheyney University.

"Correct student number one." The moderator nodded and smiled in her direction. To Walter he raised his bushy eyebrows and tilted his head.

"The next question in this category states: Which was the first HBCU owned and operated by African Americans?"

Again Walter was clueless, his nemesis however wasn't. She

picked B for Wilberforce University.

"Correct student number one. My, my, my, we have quite a competition brewing here. Let us review the scores: Chicago's The Westside Academy has earned eight points and so has Rockford High. We are at a tie with only four more points remaining. With the competition heating up, I feel the next category is quite fitting: commerce, or the Capitalistic arena of business. Question one: Who was the first African American CEO of a Fortune 500 company?" Walter pushes B for Franklin D. Raines and knows he has the points. His nemesis pushed A for Richard Parson.

To her Walter whispered, "Your guy was 2001 Time Warner; my guy was 1999 Fannie Mae Corporation."

"Whatever," was her reply with eyes forward.

Last year, Walter had to do a paper in Civics about the moral responsibilities of CEOs. While researching the topic, he got curious about if there had ever been a Black CEO. He found out about Richard Parson and later Franklin D. Raines.

"The tie is broken. Congratulations student number three." The moderator's nod and smile went to Walter.

"All right, let's go Walter!" came from the audience.

Surprised at the outburst but happy to hear it, Walter looked to the audience and sees Coach Williams standing alone and clapping. "Let's get it done!" He yelled while clapping his hands in the air. Walter couldn't help but to laugh as Mindy pulled Coach Williams down to his seat.

"Final question young scholars: What was the first publically traded African American owned and controlled company?" Walter pushes A for Black Entertainment Television, but didn't get the point. Student number one from Rockford High pushed her button first.

"Oh my, my, my. This is the first time in the Bowl's history that we will split the points evenly, and the first time in ten years that all the questions have been answered correctly. And this is the first time ever that we will have to award first place medals to two different schools. That was outstanding young scholars simply outstanding. Congratulations!"

The moderator stepped around his podium to center stage and applauded both Walter and his nemesis. The audience roses to its feet and joined in his applause.

Walter heard whistles and loud yells from both Coach Williams and Mindy. He saw Mr. Pratt giving him the thumbs up and mouthing, "I told you. I told you, you could do this." He saw Jason stand and walk toward the exit.

The moderator pulled both Walter and the Rockford student from behind their podiums to center stage. The applause felt good to Walter, and so did center stage. He looked to the Rockford student and saw her round eyes tearing. He looked away because he didn't want his eyes to tear. The moderator held both of their hands up, and the crowd cheered.

Walking down the stairs exiting the stage, the Rockford student who was front of Walter turned her head to face him and asked,

"What colleges have you applied to?"

"None," was Walters reply, "college is for smart kids."

"And what are you?" she asked once she got to the bottom of the stage steps facing him.

"I'm just a regular kid who likes to do a little stuff on the

Internet."

"Doing stuff on the Internet is called research which is a scholarly activity, and smart kids enjoy it. I am an honor roll student and have been since the sixth grade, and you almost shut me down. If I were you, I would consider applying for college because you are a smart kid."

He was about to thank her for the compliment, but her teammates and supporters pulled her away. He saw Mindy, Coach Williams, and Mr. Pratt at the exit door waving to him.

When he got into the corridor, the moderator of the Bowl approached Walter and handed him a card and said, "I recruit for Howard University. We would be very interested in beginning conversations with such an astute young man as yourself Mr. Smith." He raised one bushy eyebrow, nodded his head, and turned to walk away.

While looking at the back of the recruiter's tweed jacket with the card in his hand Walter asked, "What does astute mean?" The moderator looked back over his shoulder and answered, "It means smart."

"Hmm," was Walter's reply.

- SEVEN -
THE PROCESS

Last year, after her mother died, she stopped believing in God. But this rejection of providence does not stop her from screaming, "Sweet Mary Mother of God . . . this damn thing hurts" as she collapses half naked into my director's chair with her left hand cupping her jaw. "That quack gave me Tylenols 3s, but they're not doing a damn thing for me."

She rocks forward in the chair and her red hair drapes her blue jean covered knees. The yellow flip-flops I gave her at the beginning of the semester are on her tiny feet exposing her manicured pink toes. She rocks back in the chair and then forward again. She is topless with her bra dangling from her thumb, and I am trying not to look at her small dancing breast, but I am looking. Not like I am attracted to them, but I am looking because they are bouncing and circling around as if they could leave her chest if they so desired.

"Damn, this throbbing . . . oh my god . . . if it would stop then I could think." She brings her right hand up to cover her left, and now she has both hands and her bra cupping her jaw.

Sitting across the concrete walled dorm room on my unmade bed, which I made earlier this morning, I am trying to decide if I should go give my best friend a comforting hug or stay seated. My mind is questioning the action because Megan is predictably violent when she is in pain or angry, and she has done much worse than swear Sweet Mary Mother of God when hurt or mad.

My eyes move from her to my new black Swiss Army book-bag, which is sitting in my lap. I start flipping the zipper with my index finger, and without looking from the zipper I tell her, "I have some Vicodin left from stepping on the nail. You are more than welcome to them." This offer isn't made without consideration. There are only seven Vicodin pills left from the prescription, and I have been using them selectively. The pills have gained value with me.

I stop flipping the book-bag zipper and look up for Megan's answer. My friend's hanging red hair is in a column of morning sunlight. She is moving her head to and fro from naked shoulder to naked shoulder.

She does not stop swaying her head nor does she raise her head to answer me, "No, those pills had me peeing on myself last time." "Well baby, that's because you did Tequila shots with them . . . against my advice I might add."

She lifts her head and opens her green eyes with red whites and places them in mine. "Really Francis? Right now you are going to go through a 'I told you so thing' with me. Do you know how fucking bad this tooth hurts? No, of course you don't. You have never had a cavity. You have never had braces. You have never had a filling. You have no clue about the pain I am feeling. You know what, yes please . . . go get the freaking pills."

She blows an exasperated breath and sits back in the chair extending her little feet and keeps her eyes on me.

I lower my eyes from her evil gaze and remind myself that she is hurting, and that's why she is being a bitch. The pills are in the small pocket of my book-bag, pulling out the pill bottle I toss it over hoping she catches it because I am not going near her.

She lets the pill bottle land at her toes, "What, you carry them around with you?" Not waiting for my answer she picks the pill bottle up, uncaps it, and shakes two into her palm.

Yes, I carry them with me because they make painful moments throughout the day better. Moments like this one go a little better with a Vicodin. Now there is only five left in the bottle anyway, and when they are gone they're gone.

I blow out my own exasperated breath and push my book-bag aside and against my better judgment rise up from the twin bed. I bend down to floor and pick up my bottle of spring water and walk my open half emptied bottle of water over to her . . . only because I love her.

She pops the pills on her tongue, takes the bottle and gulps the water, "Thanks. There is no reason for anything to hurt this bad." She lowers her head and exhales again, "When I called my father to tell him about the dentist not taking our insurance, he told me his last tooth ache hurt worse than passing a kidney stone. I laughed, but know I believe him. This whole side of my face hurts, no," she cresses the left side of her face, "this whole side of my head hurts, and I swear the pain is moving down to my neck. I wanted to go to class but walking spreads the pain. I barely made it down the stairs to your room. " She raises her head to see me looking down at her, "Thank you for the pills."

She tries to hand me the water bottle back, nope. I know where Megan's mouth has been, at least some of the places, and I am not drinking behind her. Her fellatio skills have been a topic on this campus since our freshman year. And besides, her toothache might be due to an infection, which she can keep to herself.

"Take the water."

"No, you keep it. What are you going to do now?"

"Find a dentist when the pain subsides and I can think." She puts the water bottle on the floor and leans back in the chair, closes her eyes, and returns her left hand to cupping her jaw.

With the school dentist not accepting her insurance, she is going to have drive to the city.

"You might have to drive to the city."

"Don't care. I'll drive back home to Dayton, Ohio if I have to."

"Didn't Dr. Leopold warn you about missing another class?"

"Dr. Leopold will have to understand; if not, fuck him and the whole Biology department."

She is in so much pain, I wonder, "Megan?"

"What?"

"Did you pray?"

Prayer helps me when I am hurting, and I know she is hurting not   only from the tooth but from her mom dying as well. We have never talked about it, not before and not after the funeral, and I have tried, but she always pushes past the conversation.

"What?" She opens her eyes and slowly sits up in the chair, "Are you deliberately trying to stress me out? I came down her to relax . . . to get away from my babbling roommate, and now you are tripping too. Don't you people understand that I am in fucking pain? Damn." Perhaps my timing isn't right, and I don't want to upset her, but Jesus does help.

"No. I don't want to upset you. I was just thinking prayer would help."

"Prayer will help huh? I am dealing with real pain here; the delusion of prayer will not help me. Did you pray about being gay?"

"What?"

Damn it, my eye is twitching. I close it halfway to stop the involuntary movement. If she sees it jumping, she will know she has upset me, and that will fuel her on. She lives for conflict.

"Did you take that to Jesus? Did you ask your god to stop you from liking men?"

"Being gay hasn't caused me any physical pain, and what does my praying have to do with you praying?"

"I'm just saying; if it can help me, surely it can help you with your little problem. And what are you talking about no pain? You were in plenty of pain less than a month ago because of being gay."

"What are you talking about? God accepts me as I am, Ms. Megan. As he made me, I don't have to pray for him to change me."

I take a deep breath in through my nose, so she can't hear me, and I blow it out through my nose as well. I don't want her to know she's getting to me. If she thinks I am calm, she will stay calm.

"I don't know about your god accepting you, but I know I did. After you came out, and all your choir and church friends on campus dumped you, it was not you and your god sitting up in here making plans to kick a their asses; it was me and you. And it wasn't your god who put on a ski mask with you and shaved Righteous Rachel's head. It was me. And you felt better after we did it, didn't you? I know you did because I had to stop you from stomping Rachel's shaved head in. Did you pray then, after you beat her bloody?"

"Shhh, somebody might hear you." She has me grinning.

Yes, it is good to have a violent vengeful ally. I put my hand on her naked shoulder and grip it firmly. She did have to stop me from seriously hurting Rachel. Once I started kicking her, I couldn't stop. Whenever I pass her on campus, I still get a strong feeling of satisfaction. Sometimes I go out of my way just to see her. Her hair hasn't grown back yet. She looks like a rude chicken, and I have to bite the inside of my jaw to stop myself from laughing at her.

"Well, if somebody does hear us then pray that your god can get you out of trouble, and while you're at it, pray for a boyfriend because I think you need to get laid, bad. Now, leave me alone. I came down her to get some rest. My roommate is upstairs crying about her damn hamster dying. And why are you back from class already? Didn't you have a lap?"

She leans back in the chair and closes her eyes. I guess she's done being a bitch for now. My attention goes to a small bundle on the floor in front of the dorm room desk.

"The TA didn't show up. Is that your t-shirt on the floor?" I point to the bundle.

"Yes, I got real hot in my chest and back, so I took it off but then I caught a chill. I'm telling you nothing has ever done me like this before. I was in your bed under the covers and about to fall to sleep when the tooth and my bra started bugging me, so I took the bra off, but the fucking tooth had me cross eyed with pain."

"Are the Vicodin working?"

"Yes, a little, the throbbing has stopped."

I walk over to the desk and pick up her t-shirt and sit in the wobbly chair the school provided.

"Beth loves her pets, Megan; you know that. She has had that hamster for two years, so of course she is upset."

Her eyes are still closed, but she looks like she's listening.

"It's a rodent. She is crying her eyes out over a pet mouse, and she is 19. Little kids cry over dead hamsters not pre-med majors who dissect small mammals. She was doing all that crying for attention. You should have heard her screaming when I flushed the carcass down the toilet. You would have thought it was a blood relative."

She didn't say that. I must have heard her wrong.

"You flushed it down the toilette?"

"Yes, what else was I to do with it: bury it or pray over it?"

"People grieve differently, Megan. Who are you to deny her the process, her process?"

"Process my ass, she was getting on my damn nerves and making my tooth hurt. I didn't do all that shouting and crying when my mother died, and this girl was crying her eyes out over a ball of fur. It didn't make any sense to me, so yes, I flushed it down the toilette, and I slapped her to calm her hysterics."

No, she didn't.

"You slapped her?"

"I had to, she wouldn't stop screaming."

She is still sitting back in the chair with her eyes closed and speaking very matter of fact.

"After you flushed her hamster down the toilette?"

"I disposed of a rodent carcass."

I put her t-shirt on the desk and sit erect in the chair.

"So, you flushed her hamster down the toilette, slapped her, and left her in the room crying."

"Yes, and came down her to relax, but that doesn't look that it will happen this morning." She opens her eyes and turns her head to face me, "Not with you being all Chatty Cathy."

Understanding is needed here at least for me. So, I push on despite her annoyed gaze.

"Why did her crying upset you?"

"Because it was continuous and pointless."

"Pointless?"

"A mouse died."

"It was a loss for her, death."

Now she sits erect, and the look on her face tells me my ten-year friend is readying for battle.

"I had a loss, a death, and I didn't perform as she is doing. My mother died. My mo – mo – mother died. And I felt no need to ball like a brainless, emotional, spoiled child. And she shouldn't either. Fuck her. What gives her the right to cry like that over a mouse, over a fucking mouse . . ."

My best friend slumps forward in the chair and starts trembling from head to toe.

Before I can get to her, she burst out in tears and wails, "My mother is dead, and that bitch is crying over a fucking rat. Yes, I slapped. I wanted to kill the stupid slut."

When I get to her, I bend down to my friend and hug her as I tight as I can and let her cry, sob, and moan. I want to tell her Jesus loves her, but I don't. I hold her tight because I love her.

- EIGHT -
INTERVIEW WITH A KILLER

The Tuesday morning's headline is startling, 'Dawes to be Executed, first in Illinois since 1999,' the sub headline reads, 'first ever to be carried out in the Metropolitan Correctional Center.' I lower the paper to the table. Maxine is a social worker there. I pick up my coffee mug and take small sip of the green tea Nancy just fixed me. An interview with Dawes will sell, and sell well. Through all the protests and media coverage, he has not granted one face-to-face interview.

"What do you think about me interviewing William Dawes?"

Nancy rolls her brown eyes up at me quickly then back to her oatmeal, "The killer?" She brought her own oatmeal, refusing the bacon, eggs, and English muffins I have in the refrigerator.

What other Williams Dawes would I be talking about, "Yes the killer, but he was a policeman before he killed." I sip the tea again. "Ok then, the policeman murderer? How would you interview him?" She is mixing the melting butter into her oatmeal. She came to the small kitchen table half nude. Seeing her breast in the morning pleases me. We've been dating for six months, and I am nowhere near my usual six-month boredom; everything about her still excites me. We celebrated or anniversary last night which included her staying over.

"What do you mean how? I ask questions he answers . . ." I put the mug down.

She looks up, "Ok, what I mean is how will you get around his overt hostility towards the media. He has not granted one interview?"

"That was before he had a date of execution. I would imagine an attitude change occurs when one knows their exact date of death." She presses her lips together which is her tell for thinking, "Mm, that could be, and if you got the interview, it would sell." She loads her spoon full with oatmeal and slips it into her mouth. I hate oatmeal, but I love watching her eat.

"How about your customer, ex-boyfriend, boss connection? Do you think he would buy it?"

"Huh, I don't know; he was looking, but he hates you, but . . . I hear he has tried every avenue available to get a reporter to Dawes. Yep, he would buy it in a heart beat and pay premium."

Her ex started as one of her weed customers then she got a temp assignment were he was and is the boss. He hit on her, but she didn't like him enough or trust him enough to get intimate, but she did go to a bunch of plays, dinners, and movies with him. When I met her, she was out with him.

"He only hates me because of you." I smile at her.

She smiles back, "You did steal his girl."

The smile shows only the tips of her very white teeth. I lean towards her and we kiss. I pass my thumb over her nipple. She giggles and jiggles her breast. I do love morning sex.

I couldn't afford a lake view, not while freelancing and working as an adjunct at Columbia. The view from the bedroom is to the west, and looking out I see the Metropolitan Correctional Center in the distance. I run two blocks beyond the prison every morning for coffee. Nancy being here stopped my morning run. She doesn't like me drinking coffee.

This will be the first execution in the MCC's history. I should shower before I call Maxine; I sound more alert showered. Sitting back on the bed, I rub Nancy's flat stomach and kiss the tip of her nose. The nose is safe if I go near her lips we might go back at it; we turn each other on something fierce. I reach over her to the end table and my phone.

Maxine is my bother's wife. We are cordial with each other, nothing more. She doesn't like me being unapologetically gay, and according to my brother she was upset because she couldn't tell I was gay by looking at me. She kept going on about him hooking me up with her younger sister until he told her that I had no interest in dating her younger sister because I liked men. She was shocked and still hasn't quite accepted the fact that her "gaydar" failed her.

She answers on the second ring, "Good morning, Jackson."

"Maxine."

"How can I help you this morning?"

"Maxine . . . this call could be a friendly greeting. Why assume I want something?"

"Because you do. In the five years I have known you, three of which I have been married to your brother, you have never called me with a good day greeting, so how can I help you?"

I want to hang up because it unnerves me to be obvious, but I need an in, "William Dawes?"

"Damnit, your brother told you he was on my case load, didn't he? I told him to wait until I had approval. When did he tell you?"

"I'm sorry?"

"You brother can't hold water when it comes to you. The man loves you to a fault. Ok, Dawes wants to talk to a Black reporter, not a TV reporter, but a newspaper reporter. He doesn't want any pictures taken, so no photographers. He wants his words to be on the mind of the public, not his image, and those are his words not mine. I think he should have forty-five photographers in here. When I told this to your brother, he suggested you because of Nancy's newspaper connection. By the way, how is he, sorry, she doing?"

That was a jibe at my sexuality and I know it, but I don't respond because I do need her. Once Maxine found out Nancy was born male she stopped hugging her and kissing her on the cheek, and she stopped the double dates we use to go on.

To be clear that I have a valid reason to be getting happy, I ask, "Henry suggested me for what exactly, Maxine?"

"Dawes is requesting to speak to a reporter, and I just got the ok this morning. I was going to have your brother call you this afternoon, but as usual he jumped the gun."

"I can be there within the hour."

"That will be fine."

I click the phone off and say, "God is good."

"All the time," comes from Nancy. "What did Malcontent Maxine have to say?"

"You are going to slip and call her that to her face one day."

"I hope so, well what did she say?"

"Dawes wants to grant an interview to a Black reporter, and my brother suggested me because of your newspaper ties."

"Wait, before you called her, you were already lined up for the interview?"

"Pretty close because of my brother and you. How sure are you that Mr. Uninformed will buy the interview?" I call him that due to him not knowing that Nancy was born Nelson.

"He is not uninformed. He is deceived, and he is miserable because he thinks he lost me to a freelance reporter with very little money and no car." She rolls closer to me and places her head on my naked thigh. "He'll buy the story, have no worries."

At the Metropolitan Correctional Center, I have emptied my pockets into a little green plastic bowl, and I put it and my belt on a moving conveyer. I raise both hands as ordered, and an officer passes over my body with a security wand. These suit pants are not the best fitting, and I have a real worry of them sliding down especially with my hands in the air. I guess the wand isn't good enough because another officer comes and pats me down. I purposely put on a suit and tie to look more professional, but I am still getting the gangbanger, terrorist treatment.

"Walk though the detector straight head and keep your arms above your head."

God please keep my pants up.

Through the detector gate an officer hands me the green the bowl and asks, "The reason for your visit today, sir?"

"He's with us officer."

I look up from the green bowl and see Maxine with two officers. I grab my belt and frantically start putting it on because people are behind me and the line is moving. I get all my belongings back where they belong and follow behind Maxine.

Quietly into my ear she says, "Cheap suit. I thought your kind dressed better."

It is a cheap suit; I got two for $175, but they are functional.

"Just trying to fit in and look the part of a civil servant, like you."

"Funny, this is an Anne Kline suit, you deviant. You won't be able to take in your notebook, ink pen, or phone. You can use you digital recorder."

"Why no notebook and pen?"

"Because those are the rules." She said with finality.

We get to a bank of elevators and one of the officers inserts a card and enters a code. They haven't spoke to me, so I haven't spoken to them. The doors open immediately.

There are no floor markings on the elevator panel. The officer inserts his card again and enters his code. The door closes and we begin to go up.

"I hope this interview helps. I believe the protestors are helping. They raise a valid point; he is being railroaded. Hopefully your interview, story will bring additional light to that fact."

"But, he plead guilty."

"I know that, but that doesn't excuse the speed in which they are executing him. My God Jackson, the shooting only occurred five weeks ago. Arrest, trail, conviction in a little over a month that is extreme. Not to mention executing him here in a federal institution that has never housed an execution. It is all madness."

She has a point, but any race conscious person knows why the rush is on. The powers that be in this country want the event out of America's consciousness as soon as possible.

We exit the elevator.

"He refused council and threw himself on the mercy of the court, Maxine."

"There was no mercy, Jackson. None."

We are in a long white corridor with no office doors or windows. At both ends are doors; we are walking to the left.

There is no handle on the door. I see a card entry slot, but the officer doesn't slide a card in. The door opens with a swoosh, and I follow Maxine in. We enter a tight six-foot square gray concrete room that has a ceiling to floor fence for a far wall. The officers remain by the entry door; I follow Maxine to the gate in the fence. There are two officers at a desk behind the fence. One comes to the fence and Maxine slides her identification throw a small opening.

"Give him your ID." She says to me.

I retrieve my license from my wallet and hand it to him. He clips both our ID's on a board, and opens the gate.

"Please raise you arms," the other officer directs and he pats us both down with Maxine's being just as intrusive as mine.

The officer with the clipboard and our ID's says, "This way Ms. Roberson and Mr. Roberson." I am sure I have seen him at my brother's and Maxine's cookouts, but again he didn't greet me, so I didn't greet him.

"I have to be with you during the interview per Dawes request. He wants a witness to what he says."

"I understand."

She could have told me I had to do the interview on my head with my legs crossed, and I would have said ok. Walking through the protesters and media to enter the MCC, I realized that this interview is going to be a game changer. Maxine is doing my career a greater favor than I understood this morning.

The officer opens a door to what I imagine is a staff meeting room because there is a meeting table with six chairs. I am relieved because I didn't want to do the interview in a cell.

In the furthest chair, I see a man whose face has been beaten beyond human recognition; there are lumps and burses and cuts covering his whole head. The sight of him makes me weak at the knees, and I collapse. The officer grabs me stopping me from hitting the concrete floor. Dawes looks like "Thing" from "The Fantastic Four."

I sit and exhale. Looking at him, the whites of his eyes are not visible; swollen flesh has hid them and the openings in his nostrils. The man's upper lip is as fat as a Polish sausage.

"Who has done this to you?"

"Which part? The arresting police swelled up the back of my head the day of the shooting," he exhales. Talking is obviously a chore, "my skull is fractured and it well remain swollen the rest of my life, my short life. The knots on my forehead are the compliments of a blanket party I received when I was on the bus getting transferred here. The fresh bruises you see on the front of my face happened two days ago here. The power on my floor went out while I was asleep. I woke up to getting my ass whipped by ghost because there is no record of any one leaving their cells or assigned posts," he takes several labored breaths.

I look to the guard and Maxine, and both lower their heads.

"Why did you refuse a photographer?"

"I didn't."

I look to Maxine.

She opens a folder and slides me a piece of paper. It is a typed statement with Dawes signature requesting an interview with no photographers. I slide it back to her with no comment. I am beginning to understand why I was granted the interview; I doubt my brother had anything to do with it.

Maxine's bosses needed a pion to interview Dawes, someone with no real media pull, someone who would not insist on a photographer. They needed someone who would look impartial and who could be manipulated. I am certain they already have media sources lined up to accept and publish the interview. I am being played.

"Will talking bother your injuries, Mr. Dawes? If so, I can come another day."

He chuckles, or at least I think he is chuckling, "Don't have too many days left, young fella. Let's get it done."

He's right. I don't know what I am thinking. He has two days left to live.

"Yes, sir. My first question comes after watching the videos of the shooting. I don't know if you aware they have released two more videos from two different angles and each shows you standing over the young man emptying your revolver and continuing to pull the trigger after the chamber of your gun is empty. At no time Mr. Dawes did you claim innocence, not that you really had the opportunity to claim innocence, but a guilty plea, sir. Why not another plea?"

He grunts and exhales, "Because I shot him. He reached inside his jacket and I shot him. Caught him in the arm with the first round. All I asked the boy to do was step aside, to clear the doorway so the ambulance drivers could bring the pregnant lady out. He spat in my face and told me, the nigger ain't been born yet that could give him orders. Mind you, I am in my full police uniform. I say, Sir, please step aside. He answers with fuck you and the pregnant black bitch and reaches inside his jacket. I pull my gun and shoot him in the shoulder. He his still holding his weapon and gets off a round that wounds my partner. I hit him in his other shoulder and he goes down. I go over to him to kick the gun out of his hand, and he fires again hitting me in the neck. I get right above him and shot his ass to death. I plead guilty because I meant to kill his ass.

"My wounded partner, grabs me from the back and wrestles me to ground and cuffs me. My partner, my partner of seven years does this; my partner who witnessed the whole shooting does this.

"When a sergeant got on the scene, I was cuffed and mad as hell about it. He asked me what happened, so I told him I killed the white motherfucker. Maybe that wasn't the smartest thing to say to white man, but that's how I felt at the moment. My white partner had cuffed me, and a white sergeant was asking me what happened, so I told him; "I killed the white motherfucker." And of course that's the sound bite the media got." He pauses to take in several long breaths. "They played the tape of me saying, I killed the white motherfucker - while showing the video of me standing over the boy shooting him dead."

I saw the loop, and that pretty much convinced me that he had lost his mind. The video loop convinced most of America and me.

"Shit, nobody wanted to hear a damn thing I had to say after that. I was a Black man standing over a white boy firing bullets into his body; I was not a cop reacting to being spat on, shot at, and shot. Nope, I was just a Black man who was shooting a white boy. I was fucked . . . and I knew it."

He stops talking and breaths. I am taking in everything he just said. I look over at Maxine and see no empathy; she almost looks annoyed being here.

"I have been a policeman in this city for twenty-three years. I know how the system works. I didn't think I was going to make lockup."

I exhale and try not to sound to angry, because I have become pissed. Not hearing his side of the story, I just assumed he snapped and killed a white boy, but "It sounds like a justified shooting to me, why plead guilty?"

"Boy you ain't listening. My partner grabbed me from the back and cuffed me. I knew what this system was going to do to me; there wasn't any sense in taking my family through all of that. What I am hopping . . . is that this interview will get my pension to my wife; hopefully, you can get some of them Black organizations together and get my benefits to her. If you can get the truth out that will help her. They gonna kill me, so they are getting what they want, but I am hoping this story . . . this truth . . . will get me a little bit of what I want. So what you think, young fella?"

I am thinking maybe Maxine didn't play me, and that they do need Nancy's connection and me. If I can get the story in one source others will pick it.

"Why did you refuse interviews before?"

"The lie was too strong to fight, the image of me standing over that boy and shooting him painted me as a racist."

I ask Maxine, "No way to get a photographer in?"

"I doubt it; I got that signed statement from my boss this morning with the approval for the interview. If Mr. Dawes didn't sign that letter that means those above don't want him photographed, and they are willing to lie to make that happen. I have done all I can."

I exhale and stand to leave because I cannot stand to look at the beaten Mr. Dawes any longer, and I have all I need for the interview, "I will get the story out, and get your last wishes to the media. I agree that enough exposure can make a difference. I have another question, Mr. Dawes; are you afraid?"

He looks up at me through those slits of flesh, "Of what, boy? Dying? Not really, I believe in God and an afterlife. My God saw what happened, and he knows my heart. No boy, I ain't afraid."

"You requested a Black reporter because of your mistrust of the media?"

"I just requested to talk to the press, been asking for a week. I thought they beat my ass to stop me from asking, but you are here."

"Your lawyer?"

"Not after the guilty plea, I couldn't tell you his name."

Catching the elevator down with the officers, Maxine says, "That was the most he said since he's been here."

I don't answer her because she's not right. Maxine is part of this man getting railroaded, and so am I. But, they made a mistake because I am going to blow his story up. I swear to God every person in America will know this truth.

Outside, walking through the protesters, my cell phone rings and vibrates. I instantly recognize the number as Nancy job.

"Jackson Roberson?"

"Yes."

"You have an exclusive interview with William Dawes for sale?"

"I do."

Pap! Pap! Pap!

Someone is shooting. Protesters start running and so do I. More shots are fired.

Pap! Pap! Pap!

I feel two hot stabs in my back and a hammer hits me in the head and drop to my knees . . .

- NINE -
LAB COAT REQUIRED

They are the only two girls in computer lab, and they are not friends. Christine attempted a friendly conversation on the first day of class, but the forced smile on Madelyn's brown Barbie Doll face crushed that beginning.

Christine is not one to extend herself, especially to girls like Madelyn who put how they look ahead of everything else. Case in point, there is only one sink in the bathroom, and Madelyn has been using the mirror to apply her make-up for the entire ten-minute break. Christine entered the bathroom to use the toilet, now she needs to wash her hands.

"I need the sink," Christine said, rolling up the sleeves of her lab coat

"You see me over here, right? And you see I am doing something, right? What, am I just supposed to stop what I am doing for you?"

Looking at her own image in the mirror behind Madelyn, Christine sees her cheeks and the tips of her ears reddening. Being larger,

Christine considers pushing past Madelyn to the sink.

"I don't know how you could do that in a bathroom with some-one else in here, anyway," Madelyn exclaimed waving her hand in front of her freshly powdered nose.

"It's a bathroom, Madelyn. That's what happens in here. Now, I need to wash my hands and you're blocking the sink."

"I need to put on my make-up, and you fouled the air. How rude was that? You are not going to bully me out of here. I have to get this done."

Christine decides pushing past Madelyn to the sink is the only solution. It won't take her twenty seconds to wash her hands. She is about to step by her until she notices a small crimson stain spreading in the seat of Madelyn's banana yellow jeans.

"I will be done here in a minute. You are just going to have to wait."

Helping Madelyn really isn't high on Christine's to do list, but she would want someone to intervene if she were in Madelyn's situation. Walking into that boy-filled computer lab would be a disaster for her. Christine can't let it happen.

"Madelyn, you should check the back of your jeans."

"What?"

"You've leaked."

"No!" She turns to see in the mirror, "Oh my God, how am I going to get that out. This can't be happening to me." Madelyn grabs her purse from the sink and starts undoing her jeans and walks to the toilet stall.

Christine steps to the sink.

"I won't be able to get this out," Madelyn gives off a sigh.

"Wear a lab coat for once. It will cover the spot."

"But, they are so drab."

"It will cover the spot."

"Yes, ok, will you go get it for me?"

"Sure, I'll be right back."

- Ten -
The Mart Man

The snapping is heavy this morning. It can be heard hitting the ground, and I sleep on the sixth level. I should have lain at the other end of the strip away from the solar shield. The solar shield is closed, but the air filtering vent is open and allowing the noise from the street to enter. The snapping woke me up.

I rarely sleep late, but this morning I'm tired. It was a busy day at the Mart yesterday, and I fared well, seventy thousand dollars in one day. Not bad for a darker one. Matter of fact, that wasn't a bad day for anyone, white ones included.

The work at the Mart is not easy, and it's even harder perpetrating as I do. The Mart is for those of privilege. I was born far from privilege. I should wear a dome on my head like others of my class sect, but I do not. This darker one walks and breaths the air as if he were of the privileged sect. I perpetrate.

If the air doesn't kill me first, I will get rich. And after my wealth is secured, I will fix my breathing parts. One has to be careful however, fatigue is the first symptom of air poisoning. I cannot afford sickness, not now. I am finally starting to make a name for myself at the Mart.

It is six a.m., an hour and fifteen minutes to open mart. I force myself out of the strip and onto my feet.

'Sleeping on the strip all day does not a billionaire make.'

That's a saying I made up while reading from one of the old paper books last month. They used a lot of motivational sayings in business during the twentieth century, not so in the twenty-first.

My plan is to earn my first billion before I am twenty-five. I will be rich before any serious damage is done from air poisoning, and whatever tissue is damaged can be replaced with cloned tissue. Besides, any serious damage doesn't happen until after thirty. And who cares what happens after thirty if one is not rich? I certainly don't. Health and wealth are parallels; neither are the worries of successful mart men. With the proper income, one has no health worries. At twenty, I live on a six level. No one else of my age group lives this high and none of my class sect. My true class sect is that of the Dome Heads.

Dome Heads dwell on sub-levels, and I don't know why one could accept that existence. It's better to breath poison air than live life with your head in a dome. Being a darker one is burden enough, but being a darker one and a Dome Head is hell.

My father, a white one, was born to privilege. The first day of his life the bio breathers were placed in his head. My mother born to a maid's aide is a darker one of the unskilled class sect. She too is a maid's aide, and never became a full domestic which would have allowed her bio-breathers. She lives her life with her head in a dome. "Damn!" the showering glycerin is over heated. I love hot showers, but not at the expense of blistering my skin. The display reads 103 degrees. It has to be wrong. When I'm done, I will call maintenance. All necessities should operate to perfection on the sixth level. The glycerin temperature is to match one's body temperature.

Could I have a fever?

"No."

The gage is wrong. I'm fine.

Toasted fruit fiber is one of the few dietary luxuries I allow myself. Everyone knows overeating is an indicator that one is from a lower sect especially the eating of flesh. My mother was not a flesh eater, but she was fond of fruits and breads. That early exposure is responsible for the indulgence I allow myself. Usually three ounces of dietary paste and eight ounces of American purified water is breakfast, but this morning, I am having apple jam on my soy wafer.

The snapping has me thinking of my mother. She made apple jam and would spread it across the surface of the breads she baked. She baked on days the snapping held us in our sub-level dwellings. It is a nice memory. Actually, it is one of the few good memories I have from life with my mother and her sect.

I do not wear a dome on my head. I use micro sponges to breathe through. I am not ignorant. The sponges do not stop me from inhaling the toxins in the air. I place a new pair in my nasal passages daily knowing they do nothing. I perpetrate in this manner because it's better than wearing a dome. And besides, who knows, the filters might catch some toxins. The idea first came to me while watching my Uncle Ray filter water through sponges for drinking.

I was ten, and had been wearing a dome since birth. That morning, I went to the store with Uncle Ray to buy water. He left me waiting in the car. A group of privileged kids walked past our car. They stopped and stared at me. One walked up to my window and asked me to take off my doom. I told him I couldn't. He looked sincere in his question, and his eyes were curious when he asked 'why.' I told him the dome was needed to clean the air so I could breathe.

He was a darker one like me. He was about to ask me another question when his friends starting chanting, "Homely domey, your mama eats bologny. Homely domey, your air is phony. Homely domey. Homely Domey." He joined in the chant and ran away laughing with his friends.

My uncle exited the store hearing the end of their chant. I asked him why we wore domes and others didn't. He told me it was the same reason we filtered our water and others didn't. The same reason we drove cars while others drove air mobiles. The same reason we lived in sub-levels while others lived above. The same reason a cold could kill us and not have others miss a day's work. The same reason our class sect worked fifteen hour days six days a week while others worked ten hour weeks. Money, those that have it live better was what my uncle told me

"Money makes men of this world privileged, but it is only the privilege of this world, Luke. In God's Kingdom good deeds build your fortune."

My uncle, a tall man with his silver dreadlocks, often spoke of God's kingdom. If I were in touch with him now, I am certain he is still talking about God's kingdom. At ten, I realized we were not living in God's kingdom.

Where we lived, money got one a life without a dome, and that life looked a lot better than mine. My Uncle asked me if I knew the kids that teased me. I told him no. He said it was a shame they had nothing better to do than to tease one with less.

One with less.

I don't know whose words repeated more in my mind during the ride home: the kid's "homely domey" or my uncle's "one with less". Neither fit well in my ten year old mind. I didn't think of myself as homely or one with less. However, I did wear a dome.

When we got home, my uncle pumped the water through his filtering system. I watched the boiling water being forced through filter sponges, and the idea formed. In my room that night, I cut two small pieces off of one of his new sponges and rolled them into tight cones and stuffed them up my nose. I had to inhale harder, but the air came through.

I had never gone outside without my dome, never. But that night, I climbed the stairs and stood before the release mat, dome-less. If I stepped on the mat, the door chamber would have revolved, and I would have been outside the air cylinder without my dome. I told myself that the worst that would happen would be me gaging and choking. But if I got right back on the mat, I would be all right.

I thought about the darker one from earlier. I thought about how he and his friends ran and played without domes on their heads. I thought about how great it would have been to run and play with them. How great it would have been to show them I wasn't homely.

However, I also thought of the stories I'd heard all my life about the suffering death that came from melting lungs, about blood running so hot inside a person that their skin blisters and eventually the blood burns through. All my life these stories had kept my head inside a dome. That night, the stories stopped me. I was seventeen when I put the warnings aside and stepped onto that mat. Uncle Ray would love this airmobile. Most American made airmobiles hover ten inches off the ground. The 2061 Falcon I drive hovers at fifteen inches and goes from 0 to 180mph in three seconds. It is the fastest American airmobile in production. The Saudi's make one faster and so do the Mexicans, but both are out of my price range, at least for now.

The snapping will have those driving gas engine cars sliding across their battered roadways. The only affect it has on an airmobile is an oily grayish buildup on the windshield. Uncle Ray said at one time the snapping was a source of water, and it was called rain. I find that hard to believe. The amount of water pulled from the snapping is minute. The majority of our water is purified from lakes and rivers. How snapping was ever a source for water is beyond my understanding. How could gray gaseous droplets that explode into oil blotches on contact with any hard surface be used for water? In China and Africa the snapping burns the skin.

Squeezing the hand held accelerator of my new Falcon reminds me of taking that liberating step on the mat when I was seventeen. The rush isn't as strong, but it definitely ignites the same mental jets. Other than the murky gray mess the snapping leaves, it doesn't cause a problem here in the city. I've been told in the rural areas where there are some sparrows the snapping kills them, and the bird's carcasses often interfere with then maneuvering of air mobiles.

We have no birds in the city other than those in the zoo habitat, so they don't interfere with the driving airmobiles here in the city. The only problem is the ancient gasoline engine cars that occasionally wonder onto the air path that runs alongside their battered roadways.

Uncle Ray often drove his car on the pathways when no air-mobiles were present. The rubber surface is smooth, and as a child I enjoyed the better ride and looked forward to his spurts of civil disobedience. But now that I own an air mobile, I understand how dangerous and foolish his acts were. I cruse at a hundred and twenty miles an hour when I have to reverse the airflow to slow my mobile down for a gasoline car, it infuriates me beyond measure. And every time it happens, it is a darker one in a dome. They have no concept of how irritating their presence can be at times.

There are none on the pathway today. I'm squeezing it up to 160 mph. Nothing feels this good to me; and that includes real sex and simulated sex. My speed is so high that the thick gray snapping residue is forced from my windshield. I've been in my Falcon less than seven minutes, and I see the bronze glow of the Mart's windows in the horizon. I reverse the airflow because blowing the Mart exit would make me three minutes late, such a blemish even a privilege darker one cannot afford.

My trainer, the only other darker one working at the Mart, had been a mart man for twenty years. His first tardy came the week after he trained me. He was fired, and they wouldn't even allow him on the Mart's premises. Conrad, a white age mate of mine who lives on a second level said the ratio is one darker one at a time in the Mart. He said my trainer was doomed as soon as I walked through the gates. I don't know if that's true or not, but I'm never late.

New to airmobiles this year is the constant hover feature. My airmobile never touches the ground. It lowers to four inches and settles. I love it. At the Mart image is everything, so I paid the garage attendant two thousand dollars for a park on the twenty-second level for a week.

Management likes it when Mart employees appear to be prosperous consumers. On the twenty-second level, I am sure to be noticed exiting my new Falcon. Next week I'll be back on twelve unless my good luck continues, and I can purchase a higher spot on a regular basis.

While on the twenty-second level, I am going to walk as slow as possible and be seen by as many managers as possible. One advantage to being a darker one is my high visibility. They can't mistake me for anyone else. Good thing I didn't miss my exit, every manager I know of is in the garage this morning. I will display smiles and nods from here to the Mart floor.

Mr. Kuhn, my section manager, is walking in my direction. He drives last year's Falcon Elite; the car is a year old, and it is still valued eight times more than my base Falcon, but mine is new.

He returns my smile and nod and briskly walks past me. I surrender the lift car to him and his assistant. His assistant's smile is one of recognition. Three years ago his knowledge of my perpetrating disturbed me. He is a friend of Douglas, the darker one of privilege, who I met as a child.

Inside my work cube, on my desk are twenty new order requests. It is going to be another great day. Last week I met a provider of melanin pills who was trying desperately to bring his product to Mart. Being a Dome Head, he is not allowed to trade, and none of the other reps were interested in working with him because they thought he could not possible deliver quality melanin pills.

Quality melanin pills offer the needed protection from the sun's rays without darkening one's skin. Seeing his desperation, and knowing how futile all his efforts would be to get Mart approval, I offered my help only with complete control of distribution. He agreed, and I got the product approved for trade. The pills were already licensed; he only needed a Mart rep.

How he, a Dome Head, got them licensed was not my concern. The pills work, and I have complete control of distribution which means all money comes to me first. His percentage is minor, but minor mart money will allow him and his donors to live better. This is a certainty. I know because I send my family a small percentage of the money earned from the Mart, and I am sure they live better; however, I haven't seen them since I stepped on the mat. One cannot be in the company of those with less when aspiring for wealth.

Many from the sect I was born sell melanin from their backs and lower thighs. My Uncle Ray would never allow anyone from our family to do such a thing. I don't see the problem with it. It is better than selling organs, which has become a booming market at the Mart. Those of privilege who can't afford cloned organs often buy organs from Dome Heads. I personally don't trade in that market. I prefer the pharmaceutical market.

The buzz is out on the floor. In less than forty-five minutes, I have doubled last week's melanin pill orders. Pharmaceutical technology is wonderful. It allows my Dome Head supplier to march darker ones into the manufactures sites and have the melanin extracted and in pill form in less than twenty minutes. With all these new orders entered in the system, my day at the Mart is almost done. I vid-mail the Dome Head to put in a new order, my warehoused supply is not gone, but the demand is great. With a couple more days like this one, it will be emptied. I feel unusually drained which is strange because after good days I'm ordinarily full of energy.

The white one Dome Head on the other end of the monitor looks stressed. He's telling me a darker one preacher is stopping people from selling melanin. I hear him, but my mind is calculating how much money can be made from the supply I have. If he cannot fill the orders, I won't be bothered with him. My time cost. He says something that pulls my attention back to the vid-screen. He wants me to come to the site. He thinks if the darker ones see me, a darker one who is a successful Mart man, they would be motivated to continue to donate.

I laugh out loud at his ridiculous idea, but the desperation in his face along with the possibilities of getting another shipment causes me to agree. This will be my last dealing with the Dome Head. This morning, I read about a new fat cream that could be spread across a penis offering added sensual girth. The cream will surely net me huge profits.

In my new Falcon, cruising at 140mph my mind goes back to taking that first step onto the mat without my dome. Life as a darker one in a dome had become too much to bear. I was seventeen, and a graduate with honors from the primary education system. No further schooling was offered for one of my sect.

Douglas, my privileged assailant had become my friend of sorts. We met again at the store, and our curiousness about each other's existence fostered a friendship. I met his family and he met mine. He tried not to act shocked at what we called a home.

He drank our home filtered water, ate my mother's bread, and sat with us in our large gathering room listening to Uncle Ray's biblical stories and his preaching of the return of the Lord. I was embar rassed for my family and much preferred spending time at his home. Within his family home, I took off my dome. And showed them all that I was not some hideous disfigured creature, but a darker one much like them. I too had aspirations and desires for wealth. My wanting confused his mother; she tried to console me by telling me it was foolish for one so restricted to request so much from life. His father also bothered by my aspirations offered me a mechanics aide position at one of his shops. His parents didn't anger me. They motivated me.

I spent many hours with his family longing to live as they did, to come and go above ground and breathe the air, to go anywhere within the city and not be restricted. His father told me if not for my dome, he would have sworn I was a born mart man. Only mart men craved wealth so. He said it jokingly, but the seed was planted.

Douglas who was going on for medical training after primary ed ucation had no interest in the Mart despite his father's urging. He was not interested in wealth for the sake of wealth. He wanted to do some greater good with his life. I thought him foolish and told him so. In response he gave me his father's endorsement letter for the Mart and dared me to go get the position.

Mockingly, he said the letter was all I would need. A letter from his father could move mountains . . . certainly it could get a 'homely domey' a position at the Mart. I took the letter and never spoke with Douglas again.

A week later, dressed in one of the hand me down suits Douglas's father gave me for church, I stood in front of the mat with my nose stuffed with water filters. My heart gushed blood to my head. I was certain death was on the other side of the airlock, but I also knew, that for me, death was on the sub levels beneath me.

It was over before I knew it. The door had never revolved as fast. I was outside above ground and breathing the air and too nervous to take a step. I stood in front of the airlock. It was the children behind me hurrying to the school bus that forced me out onto the walk. They brushed by me not noticing who I was.

I expected the air to at least sting, to stink, to make me dizzy: none of that happened. A public airmobile carrier stopped and I boarded. On it where people of privilege on their way to the business district to work. The Dome Head driver asked did I schedule the stop. I told him no. He said not to worry; he would add it in the morning. I took my seat next to others who had the conveyance of a scheduled airmobile carrier picking them up for work.

The letter of endorsement from Douglas' father worked like a charm. I was assigned a training schedule and living quarters. The only glitch came a day after training ended when Mr. Kuhn's assistant came to my living quarters. He informed me that he received a vid-mail from Douglas nullifying the letter of recommendation his father wrote. The assistant stood at the door silent. He began to unbutton his shirt, and I saw a scare that went from the nape of his neck to his waistline.

"What you want Luke, costs a great deal. Be sure you are ready to pay the price, young Mart man."

He left with our shared secrete. I assumed the scare was left from purchased lungs. That was three years ago before I proved myself as a mart man. Before I made Mr. Kuhn more money than anyone in my age group; the top producer's spot has been mine since day one. I surpassed many of those with senior standing. This darker one is valued of that I'm certain.

I bring my Falcon to a stop on the path across the street from the manufactures' site. His is the only vibrate business in the area. The buildings around him are shells emptied and gutted by the city and scrape scavengers. Nothing remains of the factories that once were but walls and roofs. I watch a group of Dome Heads donors walk to the site door.

A man also wearing a dome intercepts them. He talks, waves his arms, and they leave. I see the Dome Head I have the distribution deal with run from the site to the man who persuaded the darker one Dome Head donors away. They argue. The manufacturer pushes Dome Head who is a darker one. The darker one does not retaliate. He walks away slowly to a parked car in front of the site. I know the car.

I haven't seen Uncle Ray in years. I haven't seen my mother in years. I send money and brief notes. They are not part of my world. I don't want to see him today. The Dome Head manufacturer will have to work this situation out himself. When I reach to initiate my Falcon, I notice my hand is covered with sweat.

At home in my shower, I calculate that with today's earnings and my savings there is more than enough to get the bio-breather implants. The shower glycerin indicator reads 101.
I have a fever.

Perhaps, I should not have waited so long for the bio-breathers, but I have felt fit until today. Buying good clothes and the new Falcon seemed like worthy the priorities at the time. I lay naked and sweating across my strip. By voice command I dropped the temperature in my sleeping area to 65.

TONY LINDSAY

My mother would always wrap me in heavy covers when I got sick. Sweating like this would have prompted her to put me in blankets. I'm shivering, but my thinking is that it needs to be cold to lower my temperature. My mother would have me by her warm stove with fruit pastries baking. The pastries were a reward if I laid still and didn't complain while waiting for the fever to break. Mmm, for a second, I can almost smell the sweet heat of her stove.

Tomorrow, I'll go to Mr. Kuhn's assistant and get the name of the doctor he used. At the very worst, I may have to secure financing for cloned lungs, but it couldn't be any worst than tha . . .

In the old days, I would have put a little brandy in her hot choc-olate and not worried about her waking up, but not now. Her mother, a physician, would have a stroke if I gave her daughter a cap full of brandy; although, I put Dr. Jasmine to sleep many of Christmas eves with spiked hot chocolates, and she turned out just fine.

Because our grandbaby, Kura, is a lot like her doctor mommy, a very light sleeper, her grandma and I are standing in the doorway like two cat burglars in our own home.

Kura lost her first tooth this morning, and she knew nothing of the Tooth Fairy. But, before we could tell her the fable, we had to call her Buddhist parents because The Easter Bunny was catastro-phe; we didn't think the Easter Bunny was Christian, but they did. So for the Tooth Fairy, we called and got the ok, and now we are standing in the doorway of the baby's room checking her breathing.

"Go on in Walter, she's sleep," Pearl says leaning against me almost pushing me into the room.

I'm not convinced that Kura is sound asleep, but I take a step into the room anyway. After Jasmine graduated, she married Timothy Tanaka, and they moved to New York to practice medicine, so we converted her bedroom into an office, but with the announcement of a grandbaby, it became bedroom again, and when we found out the baby was going to be a girl, we painted the room pink and added the princess bed with all the girly amenities.

The bed is only three steps away from the door; I hear Kura's long even breaths. She is sleep. I reach into my pocket and pull out the ten dollar bill; her grandma wanted to give her a coin dollar. While reaching for the pillow, her eyes pop open.

"Hey, Grandpa Walter," she yarns, "is it time for biscuits and gravy?"

She and I have been eating biscuits and gravy in the morning for breakfast unbeknownst to her low calorie breakfast eating grandma.

"Not yet baby, I thought I heard you having a bad dream."

"Nooo," and she falls right back to sleep just like Jasmine did as a child. I slid my hand under her pillow getting the tooth and leaving the bill. I quietly back out of the bedroom.

I don't like her calling me Grandpa Walter; I wanted to be plain Grandpa, but since she has another grandpa, I have to settle for 'Grandpa Walter.' Seems to me she could call her other grandfather 'Granddaddy' or something.

Out in the hall, I show my wife the tooth and say, "Operation Tooth Fairy completed." I walk up front to my chair and television; we've only missed a couple of minutes of the news.

"She's going to remember you were in there." My wife says sitting on the sofa next to my easy chair. She tosses a throw over her lap and legs.

"No, she won't. Remember how Jasmine would wake some nights and never remember; Kura is the same." I sit in the chair and rear back causing it to recline and the leg braces to extend. I grab the television remote from the holder in the arm of the chair and push the power button.

"You think Kura is the same. She is Jasmine's daughter, not Jasmine." My wife says.

"She won't remember. Our grandbaby will wake up and see her tooth gone and ten dollars, and she will be happy."

"Ten dollars," she shakes her head and frowns, "what happened to leaving the dollar coin?"

I don't answer.

"You going to spoil her rotten. And don't think I didn't hear about the biscuits and gravy," she swings her feet up on the sofa.

"She won't remember."

"Yes, she will."

I push the leg brace of the chair down, "I got taste for hot chocolate and a shot of brandy. You want some?"

"Nope, and neither does your diabetes."

"One cup and a shot won't kill me."

"Grandpa Walter! Grandpa Walter! She came! She came . . . just like you said she would. She came and look . . . I have ten dollars!"

I wake to her big toothy smile that has a hole in it. I reach over to wake my wife and see her spot is empty.

"Grandma Pearl said that you heard the Tooth Fairy when you came into my room last night. Did you see the Tooth Fairy, Grandpa Walter? Did you see her a little bit? Did she have fairy dust trailing behind her? Where her wings like birds, butterflies, or clear like a fly? Oh tell me you saw her a little bit, Grandpa Walter." I look at the clock on the nightstand, and it reads 8:45. I seldom sleep past 6:00, but I seldom drink two cups of hot chocolate with several shots of brandy.

I sit up blinking my vision clear, "Did I see her? Of course I did."

"I knew it!" She jumps up like she has car springs in her heels.

"Settle down baby. I didn't see her when she came in; I must have been asleep, I saw after I left your room. I saw her leaving. She came in through our room because your room doesn't have a window. When she left, she went straight through the glass without raising the window, magic."
She gets up in the bed and sits next to me, "And her wings?"

"Oh, they were clear surrounded by glittery fairy dust. I tried to get some of the dust for you, but soon as I touched it, poof, it disappeared."

"Oh!"

"Kura!" My wife calls from the kitchen, "Did you tell your Grandpa Walter that the biscuits and gravy are ready?"

"Let's go eat, Grandpa Walter. We have biscuit, gravy, and ham!"

"Ok," I say, looking at my granddaughter who looks so much like my daughter.